Also available

The Mayfair Mysteries

series:

THE CASE of the Ruby Necklace

THE CASE of the Poisoned Pie

THE CASE of the Haunted Hotel

The Mayfair Mysteries

THE CASE
of the Suspicious Supermodel

Alex Carter

RED FOX

THE MAYFAIR MYSTERIES:
THE CASE OF THE SUSPICIOUS SUPERMODEL
A RED FOX BOOK 978 1 849 41173 8

Published in Great Britain by Red Fox Books,
an imprint of Random House Children's Books
A Random House Company

This edition published 2011

1 3 5 7 9 10 8 6 4 2

Series created and developed by Amber Caravéo
Copyright © Random House Children's Books, 2011
Cover illustration by Katie Wood

The Random House Group Limited supports The Forest Stewardship
Council (FSC®), the leading international forest certification organisation.
Our books carrying the FSC label are printed on FSC® certified paper. FSC is
the only forest certification scheme endorsed by the leading environmental
organisations, including Greenpeace. Our paper procurement policy can be
found at www.randomhouse.co.uk/environment

MIX
Paper from
responsible sources
FSC® C016897

Set in Stempelschriedler

Red Fox Books are published by Random House Children's Books,
61–63 Uxbridge Road, London W5 5SA

www.**kids**at**random**h**ouse**.co.uk
www.**totally**rand**om**books.co.uk
www.**random**h**ouse**.co.uk

Addresses for companies within The Random House Group Limited can be found at:
www.randomhouse.co.uk/offices.htm

THE RANDOM HOUSE GROUP Limited Reg. No. 954009

A CIP catalogue record for this book is available from the British Library.

Printed and bound by CPI Group (UK) Ltd, Croydon, CR0 4YY

With special thanks
to Narinder Dhami

Lauren

Eye colour: blue

Hair: auburn – like the rest of the family – cut into a bob

Style: jeans, T-shirts and Converse

Siblings: Charlie, an annoying little brother

Likes: anything sporty, especially swimming in the lush hotel pool

Dislikes: tidying her room

Prize possession: mobile phone, for keeping the other girls up to date with all the action at the Mayfair Park

Dreams of: running her own chain of luxury hotels, one in LA, New York, Paris, Dubai . . . a home on every continent!

Jas

Eye colour: brown

Hair: shoulder length, Afro-Caribbean curls

Style: glam and wild! Favourite items include super-sparkly shoes and anything with animal print

Likes: spending time with her BFFs

Dislikes: sitting still, Maths lessons, sitting still in Maths lessons . . .

Secret talent: impressive acting skills – useful in getting the girls out of several sticky situations with The Snoop

Dreams of: becoming the next Beyoncé or Naomi Campbell – Jas is definitely the diva of the group!

Mia

Eye colour: brown

Hair: very long, very dark, shiny and straight

Style: eclectic – Mia mostly wears bright colours, layered with one of her mum's vintage Spanish scarves

Siblings: two geeky older brothers

Likes: all animals, especially those in need of some TLC

Prize possession: a top-of-the-range laptop – Google can help solve almost any mystery!

Dreams of: working for the United Nations, or becoming a vet

Becky

Eye colour: grey

Hair: blonde, shoulder-length curls

Style: pretty and girly . . . floaty skirts, floral tops and high heels

Likes: organising things for everyone, especially her forgetful dad . . . and chocolate!

Dislikes: untidiness – the total opposite of super-messy Lauren!

Prize possession: her collection of celeb memorabilia. Mayfair Park is the perfect place for celeb-spying . . .

Dreams of: being a high-flying celebrity agent – Becky was born super-glam and super-organized!

CHAPTER ONE

'I'm just booking that for you now, Mrs Shaw,' Lauren Bond said in her most professional telephone voice. Quickly she tapped away at the computer on the reception desk. 'A double room from the sixteenth for three nights. We look forward to seeing you and your husband at the Mayfair Park Hotel then, Mrs Shaw. Goodbye.'

Lauren put the phone down and then quickly double-checked the computer to make sure that she'd added the booking correctly. She didn't want anything to go wrong because it had taken her a while to persuade her mum and dad, who ran the hotel, to let her take over the reception desk, even for just half an hour. They were short-staffed at the moment, and Lauren was just covering for one of the real receptionists, Emma, who was on her break.

Once the hotel had had a temporary receptionist who'd managed to wipe a whole week's bookings off the computer, Lauren remembered with a grin. She could just imagine her parents' faces if she went and told them she'd done *that*! Although Lauren was pretty sure that if she *did* make such a hair-raising mistake, one of her best friends, Mia, who was a computer geek, would be able to sort it out . . .

Remember to look busy, but calm and unflustered, Lauren reminded herself. That was what her dad, who managed the hotel, always told the receptionists. Smoothing down her auburn bob, Lauren began to tidy the desk, shuffling papers together and putting tops back on pens. As she did so, though, she kept a close eye on what was going on in the lobby in front of her.

The Mayfair Park Hotel was a grand old building, but it had been decorated in a luxurious, up-to-the-minute style. Lauren adored the cream and blue interior, the large squashy leather sofas, the tall plants in shiny ceramic pots and the extravagant but tasteful displays of fresh flowers.

It was early evening now, and most guests had already checked in for the night. The smart, glassed-in café-bar on the other side of the lobby was full of people enjoying a drink before having dinner in the restaurant.

Lauren couldn't believe how lucky she was living in a hotel like the Mayfair Park. Most of the staff lived off the premises, but Lauren, her younger brother Charlie and their parents had a flat in a wing of the hotel. It was *such* a great place to hang out, Lauren thought happily, and her best mates Jas, Mia and Becky agreed. They'd just broken up today for the half-term holiday, and Lauren was looking forward to spending lots of time chilling at the hotel with her friends. There was always so much going on, and so many different people to meet . . .

Suddenly the doors at the front of the hotel swung open, and a tall young woman walked in. She paused just inside the door, took off her huge black shades and glanced around.

Lauren caught her breath. This girl was *beautiful*. She had long, very wavy blonde hair, some of which was caught up with an amazing diamanté butterfly clip on top of her head, while the rest rippled free down her back. She was only wearing a T-shirt, jeans and flat shoes – the kind of clothes Lauren, who didn't like fuss and high heels, would choose to wear herself. But even Lauren could see that this woman's clothes weren't ordinary at all. Her faded skinny jeans showed off her long legs and her cropped silk

3

T-shirt had an intricate printed pattern of pink and purple swirls that drew the eye. Her flat ballerina shoes were the exact same shade of purple, and around her slim hips was a wide brown leather belt with a huge silver buckle. Lauren felt completely dazzled and couldn't stop staring!

The young woman turned her head towards the reception desk, her star-shaped silver earrings twinkling in the light. She spotted Lauren and, smiling, made her way towards her.

It was then that Lauren realized, with a shock, that she'd seen her before. But where? Lauren racked her brains for the answer, but she simply *couldn't* remember.

'Hi there.' The girl stopped in front of the desk. She was still smiling at Lauren but she was looking rather surprised, too. 'I'm Sara MacDonald. I have a reservation here for the next week.'

'Sara MacDonald,' Lauren repeated, turning to the computer. Sara was even more beautiful close-up, Lauren thought, with her deep green eyes, clear complexion and even, white teeth. 'Let me just check that.'

Sara raised her eyebrows. 'Sorry to mention it, but you *do* seem a bit young to be a receptionist!' she remarked with a wide grin.

'Oh, I'm not really a receptionist – as you've probably guessed!' Lauren laughed. 'My mum and dad run the hotel and we're short-staffed this evening. So I'm just standing in while the receptionist has her break.'

At that moment the hotel doors swung open again and a cab driver staggered in. He was carrying two designer suitcases, one in each hand, and Lauren could see that the cases looked incredibly heavy.

'I'll just get the rest of your luggage,' the driver called to Sara.

'Thank you,' Sara called back.

Quickly Lauren found Sara's booking on the computer. 'So you're staying for six nights, Miss MacDonald,' Lauren checked. 'We've allocated you Room two-o-one. I'm sure you'll find it really comfortable. Breakfast is served from seven-thirty a.m. until ten a.m. in the café-bar just behind you. And now, I'll just sort out your key-card.'

'Well, you might be a bit young to be a receptionist, but you're doing brilliantly!' Sara remarked, looking impressed as Lauren activated the key-card. 'And do please call me Sara.' She peered at Lauren's name badge. 'Hi, Lauren. It's lovely to meet you. I've got a sister called Mel who's about the same age as you.'

Lauren grinned at Sara as the cab driver tottered through the doors once more. He was panting quite heavily and was carrying another suitcase, a large vanity case and an outsize leather tote bag.

'I'll just get the last few things,' the driver wheezed.

Sara laughed as she saw the amazed look on Lauren's face. 'I know – isn't it awful?' she giggled. 'Everything but the kitchen sink! But I *have* got an excuse. I'm a model, and I've got a busy week of work – and parties! – ahead, so I need lots of different outfits.'

'Oh, are you here for London Fashion Week?' Lauren asked. The prestigious fashion event had started that very day and ran until the following Wednesday, and Lauren knew that several other models and designers, as well as people attending the catwalk shows, had checked into the hotel over the last few days.

Sara nodded. 'Yes, I'm modelling for a couple of the designers next week,' she explained. 'But I've got some other jobs on too, while I'm here in London. Tomorrow morning, really early, I've got a fashion shoot in Covent Garden for a women's magazine. But I'm going to be *really* busy because I've got several shoots lined up for the cosmetics company, Princess Pink.'

'So *that's* where I've see you before!' Lauren exclaimed. Princess Pink were a very high-profile and successful make-up brand, and they advertised in all the glossy magazines, as well as on TV. The centrepiece of all their ads was a gorgeous blonde girl with big green eyes – whom Lauren now realized was Sara Macdonald herself! 'I *knew* I recognized you.'

'I get that a lot,' Sara said with a laugh. 'People stare at me in the streets all the time, but they just can't think how they know me! That's because I'm not really a *proper* celebrity like an actor or a singer.'

'Well, I think you are,' Lauren replied. 'My best friends, Jas, Mia and Becky, are going to be *so* excited when I tell them I've met you!'

The cab driver had now brought in two smaller suitcases, and he piled them up with the other bags in the middle of the lobby.

'Thank you *so* much,' Sara said, handing him a huge tip.

'One of the porters will take your luggage up to your room,' Lauren told her.

Just then Emma, the receptionist, came back from her break and slipped behind the desk.

'Any problems, Lauren?' she asked with a smile.

'I don't think so,' Lauren replied. 'I took two phone bookings and I've entered the details into the computer, and I've just booked in Sara, our new guest.'

'She was wonderful!' Sara broke in, stowing her purse away in her leather tote. 'Thank you, Lauren.'

'Well done,' Emma murmured to Lauren. 'You're a natural!'

Blushing a little, Lauren popped out from behind the desk, leaving Emma to deal with a guest who'd just arrived to report the loss of his key-card.

'Maybe I could show you to your room, Sara?' Lauren said a little hesitantly. She *really* wanted to carry on chatting with Sara, but she didn't want to be a nuisance. Lauren was relieved when Sara's face lit up.

'Oh, that would be fabulous, thank you!' she exclaimed. 'I don't usually like staying in hotels that much, but I can see that the Mayfair Park is going to be very different, if everyone's as warm and friendly as you.' Sara smiled. 'You *do* remind me of my sister, Mel.'

The tinkling ring tone of a mobile phone

interrupted them. Sara stopped dead and pulled her phone out of the pocket of her jeans.

'Sorry, Lauren,' she mouthed, 'I just want to take this call. Shan't be a minute.'

Politely Lauren moved away to give Sara some privacy. But as she did so, she spotted two eyes peering at her through the leaves of one of the tall potted plants. Lauren heaved an exasperated sigh.

'Charlie!' she whispered. 'Come out from there – now!'

'But I'm on a mission!' Lauren's brother whispered back, still skulking behind the plant. 'I've spotted something *very* suspicious.'

Honestly, Charlie was the *absolute* limit sometimes, Lauren thought. Her younger brother was obsessed with spies and secret agents, and he was always looking for mysteries to solve with the help of his best friend and equally spy-obsessed sidekick, Joe. Lauren had to admit, though, that she'd become a lot more interested in solving mysteries herself since she, Jas, Mia and Becky had become involved in a couple of strange goings-on at the hotel. The four girls had turned detective and so far they had investigated 'The Case of the Ruby Necklace' and 'The Case of the Poisoned Pie'. Solving mysteries was addictive, Lauren thought, but the big difference was that she and the girls weren't annoying pests like Charlie and Joe!

'What's so suspicious, then?' Lauren asked.

'She is!' Charlie said, nodding at Sara who was talking animatedly on her phone.

'*Sara?*' Lauren's eyes opened wide. 'Why?'

'Well, look at how much luggage she's got!' Charlie pointed at the designer bags the taxi driver had brought in. A porter had arrived with a trolley and was loading the bags onto it. 'That's too much luggage for just one person. So what's she up to?'

Lauren tried not to laugh. Even though Charlie *could* be incredibly annoying, he *was* quite cute with his curly auburn hair, the same shade as hers, and his big blue eyes.

'Maybe she's a spy and those cases are full of all her techie gadgets!' Charlie went on eagerly.

'Charlie, Sara's a model,' Lauren explained. 'Those suitcases are full of clothes, shoes and make-up.'

'A *model?*' Charlie's face wrinkled in deep disgust. The look on his face was so comical that Lauren had to laugh as her brother walked off.

'Sorry about that, Lauren.' Sara re-joined her.

'That was my best friend Chloe on the phone. She's working in London next week, too, so we're going to meet up. She's staying at the Courtland Hotel just a few blocks away. I'm so excited!'

'What does Chloe do?' Lauren asked as they took the lift up to the second floor.

'Oh, she's a model too,' Sara replied. 'So, do you want to be a hotel receptionist when you grow up, Lauren?'

Lauren shrugged. 'I'm not sure,' she said. 'I haven't really decided. But I like meeting new people and chatting away to them, so it's good experience.'

'Oh, I love meeting people too,' Sara agreed enthusiastically, 'although I think I talk too much sometimes! I got the first Princess Pink TV ad after I met the casting director, Janet Murray, at a party. We got on really well, but for ages I didn't even realize who she was! Then she offered me the Princess Pink job, and I've been working for them ever since. It's a *really* big contract, and I get loads of work *and* loads of free make-up, so I've been very lucky.'

'Yes, very lucky,' Lauren replied. But secretly she thought that luck didn't have much to do with it. Sara was so beautiful and sweet and friendly, Lauren couldn't imagine anyone *not* liking her.

'Here's your room, Sara.' Lauren stopped outside the door of 201. 'I'll leave you to settle in.'

'Thanks.' Sara beamed at her, then yawned. 'I'm so tired! I think I'll have a shower and order a snack from room service. I'm sure we'll meet again, Lauren. Goodnight.'

'Goodnight,' Lauren replied.

Charlie was way off target this time, she thought with a grin as she headed off to the Bonds' flat. There was *nothing* at all suspicious about Sara MacDonald. In fact, the model was one of the coolest people Lauren had ever met at the hotel.

And she couldn't *wait* to tell Jas, Mia and Becky all about it!

CHAPTER TWO

'Have you seen Sara MacDonald again since she checked in, Lauren?' Jas asked eagerly. 'I'm dying to meet her.'

Regretfully Lauren shook her head. 'No, I haven't. She said she had a really early fashion shoot this morning, and I don't know if she's back yet.'

'I'd like to meet Sara too,' Becky said. 'I bet she's got some *really* gorgeous clothes!'

It was Saturday, the day after Sara MacDonald had checked into the hotel, and Lauren was hanging out with Jas and Becky in the spa tub next to the hotel pool. It was bliss sitting in the warm, bubbly water after a hard week at school, Lauren thought, wiggling her bare toes. Especially as they were now on holiday! Her mum and dad didn't mind Lauren and her mates using the hotel facilities as long as they didn't annoy the guests or get in their way.

But at the moment the huge blue-and-white tiled pool was empty except for Charlie and his friend Joe who were splashing around happily.

'Ooh, yes!' Jas agreed, stretching out her long legs. Her dark hair was knotted up casually on top of her head, a style that really suited her, Lauren thought. 'And lovely shoes and loads of make-up . . .'

Suddenly Becky burst out laughing.

'What's so funny?' Lauren asked.

'Well, here we are talking about models and clothes and all things glamorous,' Becky said with a grin, 'while at this very minute, Mia is probably up to her elbows in hay and horse poo – and loving it!'

Lauren and Jas giggled. Their friend Mia's other passion, apart from computers, was animals. She had lots of pets of her own, including a dog, cats and rabbits, but at the moment she was also looking after Sparky, her friend Suzie's horse, while Suzie was away for the half-term holiday.

'Is Mia going to come round later?' asked Jas, turning up the bubbles.

'She said she would, if she isn't too tired after mucking out Sparky,' Lauren replied.

Jas wrinkled her nose. 'Mucking out?' she repeated. 'That sounds pretty disgusting.'

'I know,' Becky agreed, shaking her blonde curls out of her eyes, 'It's bad enough clearing up after my dad!'

Lauren grinned. Becky's dad was a typical absent-minded college professor, and Becky had had to take charge of things at home ever since her mum died a few years ago. Becky was *so* clever and efficient and sensible, Lauren thought admiringly, but she was a great laugh too.

'I wonder what it's like being a model and being photographed all the time?' Jas said thoughtfully.

'*You'd* be no good at it, Jas,' Becky teased. 'You can't sit still for five minutes!'

Just then the outside door opened, and Mrs Stoop, the hotel's head of housekeeping, looked in. Lauren's heart sank a little, as it always did whenever she encountered The Snoop, which was what she and the girls secretly called her. The housekeeper was very good at her job, but she was rather a forbidding character, and she certainly didn't agree with Lauren, Charlie and their friends being allowed to use the hotel facilities so freely. Lauren knew for a fact that The Snoop had complained about it to Mr and Mrs Bond several times.

Lauren sat up abruptly and cast an anxious

look at Charlie and Joe to make sure they were behaving themselves. But the two boys were swimming up and down side by side with identical angelic looks on their faces.

Mrs Stoop didn't say anything. She simply nodded at the girls and went out again.

'Ooh, I hate it when The Snoop pops in and out like that!' Lauren complained, pulling a face at Jas and Becky. 'I just *know* she's trying to catch us out doing something we shouldn't.'

'I'm fed up with it too,' Jas agreed as Charlie and Joe climbed out of the pool. 'Maybe we should do something to teach The Snoop a lesson? I'll have to come up with a plan!'

Lauren shook her head at her. Jas was always full of ideas, some of them outrageous and downright crazy, and she always had a plan for *everything*!

'Shall I give Mia a call after we've got changed and see if she's coming over?' Becky began. But then she broke off and gave a loud shriek of surprise as a giant inflatable banana splashed into the spa tub right in front of her. Jas began to laugh but then it was *her* turn to scream as a big blow-up rubber ring crashed into the water next to her.

'Look out!' yelled Charlie. He hurled a large

yellow duck towards them which bounced lightly off Lauren's head and then fell into the tub. 'It's the invasion of the giant inflatables!'

Lauren glared at Charlie and Joe who were now almost helpless with laughter.

'You two are SO dead!' Lauren exclaimed, chucking the duck in their direction. Then, out of the corner of her eye, she saw Sara MacDonald come out of the changing-rooms, carrying her mobile phone in one hand. Sara put her phone down carefully on one of the striped sun-loungers, then stepped into the poolside shower.

'OK, there's a guest coming into the pool now,' Lauren warned the boys in an undertone, 'so you'd better behave yourselves.'

'It's that model again,' Charlie muttered to Joe in tones of disgust. 'You know, the one I told you about with all the luggage? Let's get out of here!'

Lauren breathed a sigh of relief as the two boys went off to the changing-rooms. Then she turned to find Becky and Jas staring at Sara while pretending not to.

'We heard what Charlie said,' Jas whispered, looking very excited. 'That's Sara MacDonald, right? I recognize her from the Princess Pink ads.'

Lauren nodded.

'I love her bikini.' Becky sighed a little

enviously. Sara was wearing a shiny silver halter-neck two-piece that shimmered in the lights.

'I forgot to tell you that Charlie thought he'd found another mystery to be solved when Sara arrived,' Lauren told them. 'He was really suspicious because Sara had so much luggage. Charlie thought she might be a secret agent with loads of killer gadgets concealed in her designer suit-cases!'

Sara had stepped out of the shower now. Her face lit up with a smile when she saw Lauren, Jas and Becky nearby in the spa tub.

'Hi, Lauren,' Sara called cheerfully, 'are these the friends you were telling me about?'

'Yes, this is Jas and this is Becky,' Lauren explained. 'And Mia *should* be here later, but at the moment she's busy shovelling up horse poo!'

Sara laughed. 'Lovely to meet you, Jas and Becky,' she said, slipping into the spa tub to join them. 'And do call me Sara. I feel like Lauren and I are old friends already!'

'We were just wondering what it was like being a model,' Jas said, looking curious. 'Well, I was, anyway! Do you enjoy it, Sara?'

'I love it,' Sara replied promptly. 'I get to wear stunning designer clothes and I travel all over the world – what's not to like? I do get homesick, sometimes, and miss my family. *And* it can be a lot of hard work, like any job, although not many people believe me when I tell them that!'

'Your bikini's gorgeous,' Becky said admiringly.

'Oh, thanks, it was a freebie from a magazine shoot I did last year,' Sara confided.

'That reminds me,' Lauren put in, 'didn't you say you were doing a magazine shoot in Covent Garden early this morning? How did it go?'

Lauren was surprised when Sara's face fell. 'It didn't go at all!' she replied simply. 'Something went horribly wrong. When I arrived at the shoot, there was another model there in my place.'

'Oh no!' said Jas. 'What happened?'

Sara shrugged. 'I'm not sure, but the magazine got a message to say I wasn't coming. I checked with Courtney, my agent, but she didn't know anything about any message, so there must have been some kind of a mix-up somewhere.'

'What a shame,' Becky sympathized.

'Oh, well, it's given me more time to relax before I start my shows at London Fashion Week in a couple of days time,' Sara said with a smile. 'I came back here and had a facial and a massage in the spa, so I felt a lot better about missing out on the job. And it was only a one-off anyway. I've got all my work with Princess Pink cosmetics next week too, and *that's* my biggest contract. I love working for them.'

'I bet London Fashion Week is really exciting,' Becky said eagerly.

'This'll be the first time I've ever modelled there and I'm *really* looking forward to it,' Sara explained. 'I'll tell you all about it next week. Now I'd better go and have my swim.' She climbed gracefully out of the tub. 'Great to meet you, girls. Take care.'

'See, I *told* you she was lovely,' Lauren whispered to Jas and Becky as Sara strolled away.

'Oh, she *is*,' Becky agreed.

'I really like her,' Jas added.

They all watched as Sara dived neatly into the deep end of the pool and began to swim up and down.

'I suppose we ought to go and get changed,' Becky said reluctantly as more guests in swimsuits began to come out of the changing-rooms. 'The pool always gets really busy around this time, doesn't it?'

Lauren nodded. As the girls climbed out of the spa tub, they heard the sound of a mobile phone from the sun-lounger nearby.

'That's Sara's phone,' Lauren said.

'It sounds like she's got a text,' Becky agreed. 'Maybe we ought to tell her?'

Wrapping her towel around her, Lauren went over to the side of the pool just as Sara swam towards it.

'Sara, you've got a text,' Lauren said. 'We thought you might want to know.'

'Oh, thanks.' Quickly Sara hauled herself out of the pool. 'I have to keep my phone with me all the time at the moment in case any of my work arrangements change and my agent needs to contact me quickly.'

Lauren, Becky and Jas watched as Sara read the text. But to Lauren's surprise, Sara's face instantly changed. She'd been happy and smiley when she climbed out of the pool, but now, as she gazed at the phone in her hand, she suddenly stood as still as stone, the colour draining from her cheeks. Lauren was intrigued.

'Oh, it's just a wrong number,' Sara muttered. But her fingers shook as she deleted the text, and Lauren was *sure* she could see tears in her eyes.

What on earth was going on? Lauren wondered. *Why had that text upset Sara so much?*

CHAPTER THREE

'I think I'll go and get changed,' Sara murmured. She was avoiding looking at the girls directly, they all noticed. 'I'm feeling a bit cold.'

Jas couldn't help wondering what was the matter, and she'd seen from the looks on Becky's and Lauren's faces that they were wondering *exactly* the same thing. Maybe it was really nosy to ask, Jas thought, but she only wanted to help.

Jas decided to ask Sara if she was all right. But before she could do so, someone called out across the pool.

'Hi, Sara!'

Jas, Becky and Lauren turned and saw another tall, blonde woman who'd just come in through the outside doors. She was waving madly at Sara.

'Oh, it's Chloe!' Sara exclaimed, immediately looking more cheerful. 'I'm so glad she could make it.'

'Who's Chloe?' Becky asked. Sara had hurried over and thrown her arms around the other girl, giving her a big hug.

'Sara said she was her best friend,' Lauren explained. 'Chloe's a model too. So, that text was a bit of a mystery, wasn't it? Why do you think it made Sara so upset?'

'I don't know,' Jas replied. 'It must have been something pretty bad, though.'

Sara and Chloe were now heading back towards Jas, Becky and Lauren. Jas stared at Chloe curiously as the two of them got closer. She was a little shorter than Sara and not quite so stunningly beautiful, but she had an interesting face with high cheekbones and cat-like, slanted blue eyes.

'Girls, meet my best-ever friend, Chloe!' Sara announced. 'Chloe, this is Becky, Jas and Lauren.'

'Nice to meet you,' Chloe said with a smile. 'Sara and I have been friends ever since we were about your age, actually.'

'Did you go to the same school?' asked Becky.

Chloe nodded. 'Yes, I used to help Sara revise for exams, and then she always ended up getting better marks than me. That's so typical of Sara!'

'Oh, shut up, you!' Sara giggled, linking arms with her friend. 'How did your job go today, Clo?

You were doing a shoot on the River Thames, weren't you?'

'Yes, we were modelling Aliyah Rivers' ball gowns,' Chloe replied.

'Aliyah Rivers?' Becky repeated. 'Her dresses are *gorgeous*.'

'They certainly are,' Chloe agreed. 'My favourite was a pale pink silk with pearl and diamanté rosebuds all over the long skirt. I loved it so much, I didn't want to take it off!' She turned to Sara. 'By the way, some of the models I was working with today are off to a party tonight. I thought we could go together?'

Sara hesitated. 'I'm not sure, Clo—'

'Oh, come on, don't be a party-pooper!' Chloe coaxed. 'Don't you think she should come with me, girls?'

'Yes!' all three girls said together.

Jas nodded in agreement. 'I bet you've got loads of gorgeous clothes you could wear,' she added.

'Yes, I'd love to see what's in your wardrobe!' Becky laughed.

Sara's face broke into a smile. 'Well, why don't you all come upstairs with me and Chloe and help me choose what to wear for this party, then?' she invited.

'Really?' Becky gasped. 'That is so cool!'

'Right, let's get going before Sara changes her mind,' Chloe said firmly. 'Give me your key-card, Sara, and I'll go up to your room while you and the girls get changed.'

Immediately Jas, Lauren and Becky rushed off to the changing-rooms. They chattered excitedly as they showered, towelled themselves dry and changed. Jas was so impatient, she put her socks on inside out and didn't bother to take them off again. She could hardly wait to go up to Sara's room and take a look at her wardrobe! Chloe arriving just at that moment after the mysterious text had been great timing, Jas thought as she stepped into her jeans. She and Sara were obviously very close – just like Jas, Mia, Becky and Lauren!

Chloe was waiting in Room 201 for them. As Jas, Becky and Lauren followed Sara in, all three girls let out gasps of amazement.

There were clothes everywhere. Chloe had thrown open the wardrobe doors, and the cupboard was stuffed with dresses, skirts, jeans, knitwear and T-shirts. Some of Sara's outfits hadn't even been unpacked because there wasn't enough room in the wardrobe, and they were still lying in the open suitcases on the floor. The clothes included shimmering silk and satin evening dresses in shades of blues, greens and pinks, soft cashmere sweaters in all the colours of the rainbow, lots of white T-shirts – all with different designs – sequinned mini-skirts and at least ten pairs of jeans.

Chloe and Sara both burst out laughing at the thrilled look on the girls' faces.

'And don't forget my shoes,' Sara added, pointing to the other side of the room where about twenty pairs of shoes were lined up against the wall. There were skyscraper heels as well as flats, in a dazzling array of colours and materials from cream to deep purple and shiny patent leather to suede.

'We'll be here all night trying to choose an outfit!' Becky murmured, her eyes almost out on stalks.

'I've never *seen* so much make-up either,' Jas sighed, staring at the dressing-table covered with creams, lotion, potions, eye-shadows and lipsticks. It looked like a beauty counter in a department store! Next to the make-up were piles of glittery necklaces, bracelets and earrings, some of which looked like *real* diamonds, Jas thought.

'Oh, I hope you don't think I'm a real spoilt

brat, having so much stuff!' Sara said a little anxiously. 'It's because I get *so* many freebies from designers, and of course, most of my make-up is free from Princess Pink.'

'So which outfit are you going to choose for tonight?' Becky asked, looking dazzled by all the beautiful things in the room.

'I usually like to wear a dress for parties,' Sara replied.

'Well, that narrows it down to about twenty outfits, then!' Chloe remarked drily, and the girls laughed.

Jas thought she hadn't had so much fun in *ages* as she sat on the bed with Lauren and Becky, watching while Sara and Chloe whisked dress after dress out from the wardrobe for their approval. It was a difficult decision because Sara had so many different and beautiful outfits – a lipstick-red sheath dress was followed by a simple white silk shift, which in its turn was followed by a floor-length gown of shimmering gold. Eventually, though, they all decided on a figure-hugging mini-dress covered in tiny emerald-green sequins.

'Gorgeous!' Becky said approvingly as Sara slipped the dress on and did a twirl.

While Chloe helped Sara put her hair up, Jas,

Lauren and Becky looked through Sara's shoe collection and chose a pair of strappy silver sandals with very high heels to go with the dress.

'They're perfect,' Sara said with a smile. She was now applying her make-up carefully. 'Look, girls,' she went on, 'these eye-shadow colours are from the new Princess Pink range called *Mermaids*.' She showed Jas, Lauren and Becky the glamorous gold and pink pots, each one filled with glittering cream eye-shadows in different shades of sea-greens and blues. 'They're not in the shops yet. I'm shooting the magazine ads for them next week. But I think this pale green one goes really well with my dress, doesn't it?'

Jas, Lauren and Becky nodded. They watched Sara apply the eye-shadow, followed by a slick of pale pink lipstick.

'Are there going to be lots of celebrities at the party?' Jas asked as Sara fastened her shoes.

'Oh, I think so,' Chloe replied. 'I've heard that a lot of soap stars and pop stars are going as well as a couple of *really* famous actors and actresses. Josh Tyler, for one.'

'Josh Tyler!' Jas repeated, very impressed. Josh was an up-and-coming young English actor. He'd starred in a very popular TV drama, and was now about to make his first Hollywood film.

'Josh is going?' Sara said, looking pleased. 'That's great! He and I made a Princess Pink TV ad together a month or two ago, and we got on *so* well. I haven't seen him since, but we've been emailing each other. He's really nice.'

Chloe glanced at the clock. 'We'd better get a cab to my hotel right away, Sara,' she said. 'I need to get changed too.'

'OK.' Sara grabbed her evening bag, a tiny silver clutch. 'Sorry we've got to dash off, girls. I wish you could come too, but I'll tell you all about it tomorrow!'

They went out into the corridor, and Sara and Chloe jumped into the first available lift.

'Bye,' Lauren called as the doors closed. 'Have fun!'

'We will!' Sara called back. 'See you tomorrow.'

Left alone in the corridor, Jas, Becky and Lauren exchanged envious glances.

'Wouldn't it be *fab* to be going off to a glamorous celebrity party like Sara and Chloe?' Becky sighed.

'Absolutely,' Lauren agreed. 'Instead all we've got to look forward to is an evening with Charlie and Joe!'

Jas and Becky groaned loudly.

'Come on, it's not so bad.' Lauren linked arms with both of them. 'Mum might let us order pizza from room service, if we're lucky!'

When the girls arrived at Lauren's place, they found Mrs Bond, Charlie and Joe in the living-room. Lauren's mum was taking a break from her hotel duties with a well-earned cup of tea, while the boys were browsing the net on the Bonds' laptop.

'I reckon you could dress up as a girl,' Charlie was saying to Joe. 'No one would recognize you.'

'I am NOT dressing up as a girl!' Joe retorted indignantly. 'Why can't I just wear a false beard and glasses?'

Jas, Lauren and Becky glanced at each other and started giggling.

'Oh, never mind those two,' Mrs Bond said, rolling her eyes. 'They're researching disguises for secret agents on the Internet! So, where have you been, girls?'

'Helping your new guest Sara MacDonald choose her outfit for a celebrity party tonight,' Jas explained. 'It was *awesome*.'

'It was really fun, Mum, but now we're all a bit envious,' Lauren said with a grin.

'Yes, we wish *we* were old enough to go to the party!' Becky added.

'Well, there *are* parties you're old enough to go to,' Mrs Bond said, a twinkle in her eyes. 'What about slumber parties? Becky and Jas can phone their parents to see if they can stay over, and you could ring Mia too. But tell her to leave Sparky behind!' The girls grinned. 'Then you four could have a slumber party right here in the hotel.'

'What, in Lauren's room?' Becky said, sounding a bit worried.

Jas and Lauren both burst out laughing. Lauren's bedroom was a complete tip and she was the first to admit it. Neat and organized Becky was always trying to persuade Lauren to tidy it up.

'No, I wouldn't put you through such a terrible ordeal!' Mrs Bond said teasingly. 'I was thinking more of an empty room in the hotel. The Sapphire Suite on the top floor is free at the moment.'

Jas, Lauren and Becky stared at her in complete amazement. The Sapphire, Emerald, Diamond and Ruby suites at the very top of the hotel were *extremely* luxurious and expensive.

'Mum, are you *serious*?' Lauren squealed excitedly.

CHAPTER FOUR

'Oh, now I really *do* feel like a celebrity!' Becky announced with a huge grin as she draped herself over a blue silk chaise longue in the Sapphire Suite. 'Isn't this just *the* best way to spend a Saturday night?'

'Absolutely,' Jas agreed. She was nosing around the enormous bathroom which was tiled in shades of blue and cream. 'Hey, girls, this bath's so big, I reckon we could *all* fit in it!'

'Mum said we could order dinner from room service too.' Lauren put a pile of DVDs on the circular glass coffee-table. 'We'll wait till Mia gets here, though, shall we?'

Becky nodded. 'I'm glad she's coming. It wouldn't be the same without her.'

'Mia sounded a bit tired when I phoned her,' Lauren remarked. 'I guess looking after a horse is hard work! But she said she was going for a ride on Sparky, and then she was coming straight over. She told me she wasn't going to miss the chance to spend the night in one of the hotel suites.'

'It's *so* cool of your mum to let us stay here, Lols.' Becky glanced around the Sapphire Suite. It had an almost Eastern feel, Becky thought, with its intricately carved cream furniture, deep-blue silk curtains and sofas, and thick-pile patterned rugs. Pure white lilies in a huge blue and white Japanese vase filled the air with their sweet scent.

Jas had now gone into the bedroom, and Becky and Lauren went to join her. The bedroom was decorated in the same colours as the living-room, and it had a king-size four-poster bed surrounded by flowing white silk curtains

'This is *gorgeous*!' Jas sighed happily. She flung herself down on the bed and bounced up and down on the sapphire-coloured satin quilt. Then she frowned. 'Lols, I thought you said we were going to watch DVDs in here?'

'We are,' Lauren assured her.

Jas looked puzzled. 'But there's no TV!'

Lauren grinned. She pressed a button by the bed and a cupboard on the wall in front of them swung open. A large flat-screen TV was inside it.

'Ooh, this is *fabulous*!' Jas declared.

There was a knock at the outside door and all three girls rushed to see who it was. Mia was standing outside smiling at them.

'You made it!' Becky cried. She, Lauren and Jas dived on Mia, hugging her to bits, and then hustled her excitedly into the room. 'Have you had a good time with Sparky?'

Mia laughed. 'I have, actually,' she replied. 'I hope I don't smell.'

'No more than usual!' Jas replied.

'Cheek!' Mia retorted. She pulled off her pink knitted hat and shook out her long dark hair. 'I *have* had a shower, you know!'

'How's Sparky?' Lauren asked.

Mia's face lit up. 'Oh, he's *beautiful*!' she announced. 'He's so alert and intelligent, and he looks at me with these big dark eyes like he understands *exactly* what I'm saying.'

'What colour is he?' asked Jas.

'Dapple grey,' Mia explained. 'That means he's a grey colour with white markings. And he has this gorgeous long white mane.'

'I think Mia's in love!' Lauren laughed. She picked up the DVDs and led the way back into the bedroom.

'I can't believe your mum said we could have a slumber party *here*, Lauren!' Mia said, her eyes wide as she gazed admiringly around the Sapphire Suite. 'It's *so* nice of her. And you said on the phone you'd met that model Sara MacDonald again?'

Lauren nodded. 'We helped her get ready for her celebrity party. She's got *so* many clothes, Mia, it's ridiculous.'

'Yes, her room is nearly as messy as Lauren's!' Becky added, jumping onto the bed and settling down.

'I hope I get to meet her in-between looking after Sparky!' Mia remarked. She sat down next to Becky, leaning back on the plump pillows. 'By the way, guys, I have to be at the stables early tomorrow morning.'

'Don't worry,' Becky said with a grin, 'Jas's snoring will keep you awake anyway!'

'Shall we watch a DVD first before we order food?' Lauren asked. 'I've got Isabella Duval's new film here. I know we saw it at the cinema, but I wouldn't mind watching it again.'

'Ooh, good choice, Lauren,' Becky agreed. Isabella Duval was her absolute favourite actress, and Becky had been thrilled when Isabella had come to stay at the hotel not long ago. That had been the start of their very first mystery, Becky remembered – 'The Case of the Ruby Necklace'.

All four girls snuggled down on the bed together to watch the movie. It was a bit of a weepie as Isabella Duval played a woman who'd lost her family in a car crash, but there was humour too, as, unknown to her, Isabella's character had a guardian angel who tried to keep her out of trouble. Although the girls had seen the movie before, they were still gripped as it moved towards the ending where Isabella finally got to meet her guardian angel.

Then, during one particularly emotional scene close to the end, the sound of rumbling could be heard over the uplifting music soundtrack.

'Sorry, guys,' Jas giggled. 'That's my tummy!'

Lauren stopped the DVD. 'Shall we order from room service now, then?' she asked. 'Anyone for pizza?'

'Yes, please!' Becky, Jas and Mia chorused.

'Toppings?' Lauren enquired, picking up the phone by the bed.

'Ham and olives,' Becky replied promptly. That was simple and uncomplicated, but it was her *absolute* favourite.

'Onions, peppers and sweet corn,' said Mia.

'Everything hot and spicy!' Jas grinned. 'Chilli peppers, onions, chorizo and spicy beef!'

'And tuna and prawns for me.' Lauren

grinned. 'Pizza toppings can tell you a lot about a person, you know!'

She was just about to make the call when they heard another knock at the door.

'I'll go,' Becky said, scrambling off the bed.

To her surprise, Charlie and Joe were standing outside.

'Mum said we could come and watch DVDs with you lot!' Charlie said, and he and Joe scuttled inside before Becky could shut the door.

'Are you sure?' Becky asked suspiciously. But Charlie and Joe were already heading into the bedroom and didn't reply.

'What are you two doing here?' Lauren asked with a groan.

'Mum said it was OK.' Charlie picked up the DVD case. 'What are you watching?'

'*Angels Around Us*,' Joe read out. 'A wonderful, uplifting story about a woman who doesn't know she has a garden angel.'

'*Guardian* angel!' Becky corrected him as the others grinned.

Charlie pulled a face. 'It sounds rubbish,' he complained.

'Well, you won't want to watch it with us, then, will you?' Lauren pointed out. 'I'm just about to order pizza from room service. If I get you and Joe some too, will you go away after you've eaten it and leave us in peace?'

'If we can have chips as well,' Charlie bargained.

Shaking her head at him, Lauren called room service. Then she and the others settled down to watch the rest of the film. Meanwhile, Charlie and Joe went into the suite's living-room and put the TV on in there.

'Perfect timing!' Jas remarked as the movie credits rolled and there was a tap at the door. 'That must be our pizzas.'

The girls jumped off the bed and headed into the living-room. Charlie was just closing the door behind one of the waiters and Joe was investigating a trolley covered with a white tablecloth and loaded with covered plates and cans of soft drinks.

'Yum, I'm starving!' Becky declared.

'There's no ketchup,' Joe grumbled.

'NO KETCHUP?' Charlie repeated, outraged. 'I *can't* eat chips without ketchup.'

'Look, you *promised* to have your dinner and then go,' Lauren argued. 'Just get on with it.'

Charlie poked his tongue out at her. 'I want ketchup!'

'Shall we call room service again?' asked Becky.

Lauren shook her head. 'No, they're probably *really* busy in the kitchens at the moment because it's dinner time. I'll just pop down there and grab some myself. Get stuck into the pizzas, girls – don't wait for me.'

'I'll come with you,' Becky said. 'Don't let Jas eat our pizzas, Mia!'

'As if!' Jas said indignantly. She'd already found her hot and spicy pizza and was cutting herself a large slice.

Lauren and Becky took the lift downstairs.

'We'll go to the small kitchen behind the café-bar, not the main kitchens,' Lauren told Becky. 'The restaurant will be really busy with everyone having dinner at the moment, and I don't want to get in Louis Henri's way.'

Becky grinned. Louis Henri, the hotel's head chef, was renowned not only for his wonderful food, but also for his touchy personality!

The girls came out into the lobby and as they did so, Becky saw the hotel doors swing open. To her utter surprise, Sara MacDonald walked in. She was barefoot, carrying her strappy silver sandals in one hand, and Becky could see that there were tears streaming down her face.

'Lauren, wait!' Becky whispered, grabbing her friend's arm. Lauren was already heading off in the direction of the café-bar and hadn't noticed Sara come in. 'There's something the matter with Sara.'

Lauren spun round and looked shocked to see Sara, head down, hurrying towards the lifts.

'Do you think we should ask her what's wrong?' she whispered to Becky.

At that moment Sara spotted them. She looked so miserable and distressed that Becky's heart went out to her. What on earth had happened?

'Sara, are you OK?' Becky blurted out. 'Why are you back from the party so early?'

Sara's eyes filled with fresh tears. Quickly Becky and Lauren led her over to a quiet corner where they all sat down on a sofa.

'I've had a *terrible* evening,' Sara explained in a shaky voice as she searched her clutch bag for a tissue. 'You remember Chloe said Josh Tyler was going to be there?'

Becky nodded. 'You said you'd done an ad with him, and got on really well.'

Sara nodded. 'We'd swapped email addresses and kept in touch. I *thought* we were friends. Well, I went over to say hello to Josh at the party, and' – her voice faltered – 'he got really angry with me and told me to leave him alone or I'd be sorry!'

Becky and Lauren stared at her.

'And then he walked off and left me standing there,' Sara went on, drying her eyes. 'It was so humiliating and upsetting.'

'It's probably just some kind of mix-up.' Lauren tried to console her.

'Maybe Josh was having a bad day,' Becky suggested.

'Maybe,' Sara agreed wearily. 'I think I'll go straight up to bed and get an early night. I have a studio shoot tomorrow for Princess Pink, and then my first show at London Fashion Week on Monday. I've got to look my best—'

A familiar noise from inside her clutch bag interrupted her. Becky recognized it from the pool. It was Sara's phone signalling she had a text.

Sara took her phone out and read the message. Then, to Becky and Lauren's consternation, she burst into tears all over again.

'Sorry,' Sara whispered, dabbing at her eyes. 'You must think I'm crazy! It's just that – well, I've been getting these really *horrible* texts for the last few days. I got one yesterday when we were in the pool.'

'Do you know who's sending them?' asked Lauren.

Sara shook her head. 'I don't recognize the number. At first I thought it was a mistake and the texts weren't actually meant for me. But now I don't think it's a mistake at all because they're getting really personal. Look!'

She held her phone out so that Becky and Lauren could read the message.

It's sooo funny that you missed out on that job in Covent Garden yesterday! You think you're so wonderful, don't you? Well, Josh Tyler doesn't think so, does he! Ha ha ha!

'That's really mean!' Becky exclaimed.

'I know,' Sara sighed. 'It's awful thinking that someone out there hates me so much.'

She wiped her eyes again as Becky and Lauren watched sympathetically. This was turning into a real mystery, Becky thought.

'Why don't you go up to bed, Sara?' Lauren urged.

'Oh, thank you.' Sara stood up. 'Would you come with me? It's silly, really, but I can't help feeling someone's watching me all the time . . .'

Becky and Lauren escorted Sara over to the lifts and they went up to the second floor. Sara didn't say anything more. She looked exhausted now with dark circles under her eyes.

'Why don't you put the *Do Not Disturb* sign on

the door?' Lauren suggested as she and Becky walked Sara to her room.

'You could turn your phone off too,' Becky added.

'I will,' Sara said, forcing a smile. 'Thanks, girls. See you tomorrow.'

Becky and Lauren waited while Sara unlocked the door and put the sign outside. Then they said goodnight and headed off back to the top floor.

'Poor Sara,' Lauren said. 'She's so sweet. Why would anyone want to be so mean to her?'

'I don't know,' Becky replied, puzzled. 'There was something really spiteful about that text, wasn't there?'

The two girls were so busy discussing Sara's situation, it wasn't until they reached the door of the Sapphire Suite that Lauren groaned loudly.

'I forgot the ketchup!' she said as Becky inserted the key-card.

'Maybe Charlie will have forgotten about it by now,' Becky suggested hopefully.

They went into the suite. The trolley was still in the middle of the room, but now it was piled with empty plates, apart from the two remaining pizzas. There were shrieks of laughter coming from the bedroom and Becky and Lauren raised their eyebrows at each other. They hurried into the room to find Charlie, Joe, Mia and Jas running around the room having a pillow fight.

'Oh, there you are,' Jas panted, whacking Charlie around the legs with her pillow. 'You've been ages!'

'My chips nearly went cold while I was waiting for you,' Charlie grumbled. 'I had to call Mum and tell her it was an emergency ketchup mission, and *she* brought some over from the flat.'

'Your pizzas are still warm,' Mia told them. She jumped onto the bed and bounced up and down, fending off Joe and his pillow. 'I had to stop Jas from scoffing them, though!' Then she took a closer look at Lauren and Becky. 'Is everything OK?' Mia went on with a frown. 'You two look pretty serious.'

'Yes, you do,' Jas agreed. 'What's going on?'

Charlie dropped his pillow and turned to Joe. 'Let's get out of here,' he muttered. 'They're probably going to watch another film about garden angels!'

'So what's the story?' Mia asked when Charlie and Joe had gone.

In between bites of pizza, Becky and Lauren told Jas and Mia what had just happened. The other two girls hung on their every word, their eyes widening in shock when Becky explained about the texts Sara was receiving.

'So that was why Sara looked all upset at the pool yesterday!' Jas exclaimed. 'And she's got no idea who's sending them to her?'

Lauren shook her head. 'No, it's a bit of a mystery, isn't it?'

'Yes, and I think it's something we should investigate,' Becky said, looking round at them. 'This is a new case for the Mayfair Mystery girls!'

CHAPTER FIVE

'This is a bit different from the Sapphire Suite!' Jas remarked with a grin.

It was the following morning, and Lauren, Becky and Jas were back in the Bonds' flat. Mia had gone off early to feed and exercise Sparky, and the others were in Lauren's bedroom, waiting for the laptop to boot up.

'My room has the personal touch!' Lauren joked, throwing some clothes off the bed and onto a chair so that Jas and Becky could sit down. 'Shame Mia couldn't stay, though. We could do with her computer skills.'

'It was a great idea of hers to Google Sara and see if we can find any clues about who sent those text messages,' Becky said, joining Lauren on the bed.

'I really hope we can help Sara,' Lauren sighed. It seemed like being a model wasn't *quite* so glamorous after all.

'If anyone can, we can!' Jas said confidently.

Lauren brought up the Google search page and tapped in *Sara MacDonald*.

'Wow, look at all those entries!' Becky commented.

'A lot of them look like Princess Pink publicity stuff.' Lauren clicked on several of the links, bringing up Princess Pink publicity releases and promotional shots of Sara wearing their make-up.

'Those are the new eye-shadows, *Mermaids*' – Jas pointed at the screen – 'the ones Sara showed us yesterday.'

Suddenly Lauren spotted a link further down the page.

Check out the new Princess Pink ad on YouTube before it hits your TV screens! Starring hot new star Josh Tyler and the gorgeous Sara MacDonald!

'That must be the ad Sara was talking about, the one where she got to know Josh.' Lauren clicked on the link and all three girls leaned forward eagerly.

The ad had been filmed on a beautiful sun-drenched beach with tall, craggy cliffs, flat golden sand and a deep-green sea with white-tipped waves. It reminded Lauren of Cornwall where the Bonds had been on holiday a few years ago. As the girls watched, Josh Tyler came wandering across the sand, barefoot, his dark hair blowing in the wind. He spotted a girl sitting among the rocks as the tide came in, and thinking she might be in trouble, he dashed over to her. At the last moment the girl tossed back her long blonde curls and turned to look at him.

'It's Sara – dressed as a mermaid!' Becky gasped.

'She looks gorgeous,' Jas breathed.

Sara had been skilfully made-up with the new eye-shadow colours, and extensions had been added to her hair so that it tumbled all over her shoulders like a mermaid's. Her legs were covered with a very realistic-looking fishtail of shimmering green and blue scales. Josh swept her up into his arms and kissed her lightly on the lips, but then Sara wriggled free and, smiling, dived into the waves with a flick of her mermaid's tail.

'That was fantastic!' Lauren declared as the ad finished with Josh staring out to sea.

'Josh and Sara certainly *did* look friendly,' Jas remarked.

'Can you go back to the Google links, Lauren?' Becky asked. 'I think some of them are from celebrity gossip sites.'

Lauren hit the back button, and the girls checked out some of the other websites.

'*Are Josh and Sara more than just good friends?*' Jas read out one of the headlines. '*There are rumours that up and coming Brit actor Josh Tyler and stunning supermodel Sara MacDonald, the face of Princess Pink cosmetics, have become extra-close after meeting on set to shoot the new Princess Pink TV ad . . .*'

'There's loads more of this stuff too.' Lauren flipped through a couple more websites that all said basically the same thing before she returned to Google. 'Sara said that she and Josh were just friends, though, didn't she?'

'They *must* have been good mates before last night if there are all these rumours about them being boyfriend and girlfriend,' Jas remarked. 'So isn't it strange that Josh doesn't want to talk to Sara any more?'

Lauren was scanning the links again. '*The Courtney Lee Model Agency,*' she read out. 'Didn't Sara say her agent's name was Courtney?'

Lauren clicked on the link and a biography of Sara popped up with more photos. But it didn't tell the girls much except where Sara had been born and went to school. It also stated that she'd done lots of modelling work, but that she had a very high profile as the Princess Pink girl.

'Look, Chloe works for the same agency,' Jas said, pointing out Sara's friend's photo.

'There's not much here about Sara that's useful, is there?' Lauren said with a frown, closing the laptop down. 'We don't have a lot to go on.'

'I think it's time I went home.' Becky glanced at her watch. 'Otherwise my dad might try to cook Sunday dinner and end up burning the house down!'

'I'd better go too.' Jas stood up, stretching her long legs. 'See you tomorrow. And thanks for a really glam weekend!'

'You're welcome!' Lauren said with a smile. 'And I promise I'll let you know if I hear any more interesting stuff from Sara . . .'

Lauren spread her homework out over the desk. Every half term she vowed that she wouldn't leave her holiday homework until the very last minute before she went back to school, and yet she always did. This time, Lauren decided, it was going to be different. So she was making a start that very Sunday evening. Lauren grinned to herself when she imagined casually telling Jas that she'd done all her homework – she could just see Jas's shocked face! Jas also left hers until the very last possible moment, despite Becky regularly getting at her about it.

Lauren uncapped her pen. She'd started off working in the Bonds' living-room, but then Charlie had wanted to play on his Xbox. So Lauren had moved into her bedroom – and quickly moved out again when she saw the mess on her desk. Instead she'd brought her books downstairs to one of the hotel lounges. There were several lounges on the ground floor, all furnished with comfy sofas and desks with newspapers and books for the guests, but Lauren had settled down in the smallest one. Decorated in restful shades of pale green and cream, it was the lounge she liked best, and at the moment she had all the peace and quiet she needed because there was no one else in there.

'Maths, first,' Lauren said firmly to herself, opening her textbook. She stared at the sums in front of her, but found it very hard to keep her mind off Sara MacDonald and those nasty texts she was receiving. Lauren hadn't seen Sara since last night, but she remembered that Sara had said she had a Princess Pink shoot today.

Lauren was just starting on her third sum when she heard a familiar voice call her name.

She glanced up and saw Sara standing in the doorway. To Lauren's delight, she was smiling widely and she looked much more glowing, rested and relaxed than she'd done the night before.

'Hi there.' Sara came over to the desk. 'What are you doing?'

'I thought I'd start my holiday homework early, for once!' Lauren pulled a face. 'How are you, Sara? You look great.'

'Must be my Princess Pink make-up,' Sara replied with a grin. 'I've just got back from the shoot.'

'Did it go well?' asked Lauren.

'Fabulous!' Sara exclaimed. 'I've worked with the photographer loads of times before and we get on really well. I had to dress up in a mermaid costume again, though, for the pictures. I've worn it before in the TV ad I did with Josh Tyler, and I can't move once I've got it on!'

'Was Josh at the shoot?' Lauren asked, hoping Sara might have discovered what made him behave so strangely the previous night.

Sara shook her head. 'No, he's only involved in the TV ad.' She hesitated for a moment, then added, 'Thanks *so* much for being really sweet to me last night when I was in such a mess. You and Becky were wonderful.'

'You look loads better now, though!' Lauren told her.

'Yes, it's amazing what a good night's sleep can do!' Sara replied. 'I've decided to try and sort things out with Josh, if I can. I'm really busy for the next few days, though, with my shows at London Fashion Week starting tomorrow afternoon *and* another Princess Pink shoot on Thursday before I finally go home.'

'It sounds really glamorous!' Lauren said. 'I'm *dying* to hear about everything you've been doing, and I bet Jas, Mia and Becky will want to know, as well.'

'I promise we'll have a girlie get-together with your friends before I leave,' Sara said. 'I'm looking forward to meeting Mia, and I'll invite Chloe too. See you later, Lauren.'

'See you,' Lauren called after her.

It was great that Sarah was so happy once more, Lauren reflected as she bent over her maths again. But the mystery of those horrible text messages hadn't been solved yet. Would Sara receive any more, or had they seen the last of them?

Lauren was feeling really upbeat as she skipped up the hotel steps the next morning. She'd managed to get most of her homework done the night before, and now she had a delicious sense of freedom, knowing that she could relax and enjoy the rest of her holiday. As a reward for her hard work, she'd popped out to buy herself a big bar of chocolate.

Lauren had just gone through the doors into the hotel, saying hello to James the doorman on the way, when Charlie rushed over to her. His face was full of intense excitement.

'The police are here!' he whispered.

'Why?' Lauren asked, puzzled. 'What's going on?'

Charlie was just about to explain when Mrs Bond came dashing towards them. To Lauren's surprise, her normally cool, unruffled mum looked extremely stressed. She hustled Lauren and Charlie into their dad's office behind the reception desk and shut the door.

'What's happened?' Lauren exclaimed, more bewildered than ever. 'Where's Dad?'

'He took the police up to that model's room to question her!' Charlie burst out before their mum could say a word. 'I *told* you there was something suspicious about her, didn't I?'

Lauren felt cold all over. 'What's happening, Mum?' she asked apprehensively.

'The police told us that Josh Tyler, the actor, has made a complaint about Sara,' Mrs Bond replied soberly. 'He claims he's been receiving abusive emails from Sara for weeks, ever since they filmed a TV advert together—'

'No!' Lauren broke in, horrified. 'I'm sure Sara wouldn't do such a thing.'

Mrs Bond sighed. 'I know how much you like Sara, darling. But I'm afraid there's more. Josh said he warned Sara to leave him alone at the weekend party – but yesterday his new girl-friend, Amy, received a very nasty parcel which contained a dozen dead roses.'

'Well, it can't be Sara who sent them!' Lauren declared firmly.

'When Josh complained, the police tracked the parcel,' Lauren's mum went on. 'And it was collected by courier right here from the hotel!'

CHAPTER SIX

'I don't believe it!' Lauren gasped. Before her mother could say anything else, she whirled out of the office and ran over to the lifts. She *had* to see Sara!

Tapping her foot impatiently, Lauren waited for a lift to arrive. She was about to jump in when she heard a voice behind her shout 'Wait for me!' She glanced around and saw Charlie scurry into the lift behind her.

'Mum's worried about you,' Charlie said as Lauren pressed the button for the second floor. 'She doesn't think you should be talking to Sara.'

'I *wouldn't* talk to her if I really thought Sara had done all those mean things,' Lauren replied. 'But I don't think she did. Anyway, I've got a mission for you!'

'What?' Charlie asked eagerly.

'Will you hang around at the end of Sara's corridor and come and tell me if Mrs Stoop comes along?' Lauren said. 'You know how nosy The Snoop is, so she's bound to have heard about the police coming, and she won't like it if I get involved. If you help me, I'll do all your chores for a week! What do you say?'

'Two weeks,' Charlie bargained.

'OK, OK,' Lauren agreed impatiently.

When the lift stopped, Lauren dashed out and along the corridor to Sara's room. Meanwhile Charlie stayed by the lifts, keeping a sharp lookout. As Lauren got closer to the room, she could see that the door was wide open and Sara was hovering just outside in the corridor. She looked tearful and stressed as Lauren rushed up to her.

'I just heard about the police,' Lauren panted, 'what's happening, Sara?'

Glancing into the room, Lauren saw her dad inside with two police officers in uniform. Wearing plastic gloves, the policemen were searching through Sara's things.

'The police say Josh has made a complaint about me,' Sara blurted out, looking totally distraught. 'I just don't understand why he's being so mean to me, Lauren. I haven't done anything to deserve this.'

'Well, *you* should tell the police about those horrible text messages you've been getting,'

Lauren urged her. She led Sara over to a nearby sofa in the corridor, and they both sat down. 'You've been targeted by someone too.'

'I know,' Sara sighed. 'It's awful, Lauren! I had to cancel my modelling job at London Fashion Week this afternoon because of this. I haven't told anyone what's happening except Chloe and my agent, though.'

At that moment one of the police officers came out of the room carrying a laptop.

'Is this yours, Miss MacDonald?' he asked.

Sara nodded, her lips quivering. Lauren felt *so* sorry for her.

'Have we got your permission to take it away with us?' the officer went on.

'Please do,' Sara said shakily. 'I've got nothing to hide.'

'Thank you,' the policeman replied. 'We'll give you a receipt to sign for the laptop. And it's probably best if you also keep well away from the hotel's computers for the time being too.'

As he turned to go back into the room, Sara called, 'Wait! I have to tell you something. *I* didn't send those abusive emails to Josh – in fact, I've been getting nasty text messages myself.'

'Really?' The policeman didn't sound like he

believed Sara, Lauren thought. 'What kind of texts?'

Sara took her phone out of her pocket, hit a few buttons and then passed it over to the policeman. 'See for yourself,' she said. 'I don't recognize the number, but I've been getting them for a few weeks now.'

Lauren and Sara watched as the officer scrolled through the texts, studying them closely.

'That's very interesting, Miss MacDonald,' he said at last, sounding a bit more sympathetic. Lauren felt relieved. 'We'll take some more details from you when we've finished searching your room, if that's OK with you?'

Sara nodded. Then, as the policeman went back into the room, Lauren saw Chloe running down the corridor towards them. She looked very worried.

'Sara, are you OK?' Chloe cried. Sara burst into tears at the sight of her friend and flung herself into Chloe's arms. 'I couldn't believe what was happening when I got your text! I came straight here.'

'I can't believe it either,' Sara sobbed. 'How could *anyone* think I'd send nasty messages to Josh?'

Just then the policeman came out of the room again.

'Miss MacDonald, we'd like to speak to you now about those text messages you said you've been receiving,' he stated. 'Would you come and join us, please?'

Sara fumbled in her pocket for a tissue and dried her eyes. 'OK,' she agreed.

'I'm coming with you, Sara,' Chloe said firmly.

As the police officer led Sara into the room, Chloe turned to Lauren. 'I'm really worried about Sara,' she said in a low voice. 'I can't be with her all the time because I'm working, but if I give you my phone number, will you call me and keep me up to date with what's happening, Lauren?'

'Of course I will,' Lauren promised.

Quickly Chloe scribbled down her number on a scrap of paper and handed it to Lauren, then she followed Sara into the room. Meanwhile Lauren rushed back down the corridor. She *had* to tell Jas, Becky and Mia what was going on! She was hoping that they'd be able to think up some way of helping Sara prove her innocence, but at the moment Lauren had no idea how.

'Thanks, Charlie,' Lauren gasped as she reached the lifts again. 'The Snoop didn't come along, then?'

'She did, actually.' Charlie looked very proud

of himself. 'She was *dying* to know what was going on with Sara, but when I told her Dad was there, she legged it!'

'Great stuff,' Lauren said. 'Thanks, Charlie.'

'Has Sara been arrested?' Charlie wanted to know. But Lauren had already jumped into a waiting lift, and the doors closed.

Ten minutes later Lauren was sitting in her bedroom, logging onto her MSN account on the laptop. To her delight, she saw from her contacts list that Jas was already online. Double-clicking on Jas's name, Lauren typed *Hi Jas, you'll never guess what's happened!* Then she waited impatiently for a reply.

It popped up on Lauren's screen a moment later. *Hi, Lols, what's going on?*

Lauren's fingers flew over the keyboard as she quickly described what had happened with Sara and the police. She finished with *We have to help Sara!* before sending the message. Jas's reply came back very swiftly.

I've got a plan for that! Let's start by checking out that parcel of dead roses that was sent to Josh's girl-friend from the hotel. What d'you reckon?

Lauren grinned to herself. Trust Jas to think of something. *Great idea!* she typed. *Someone must have handed the parcel in at Reception.*

Exactly! Jas bounced back. *You'd better find out which receptionist was on duty when the parcel was left for the courier. Then we can talk to whoever it was – they might have noticed something suspicious!*

That'll be easy, Lauren typed. *Going to text Becky and Mia now and ask them to get online so I can tell them what's going on.*

OK, and don't worry, Lols, Jas wrote back, *the Mayfair Mysteries girls are on the case!*

'So it was Sophie who was on duty when the dead roses were dropped off at Reception?' Jas asked in a low voice as she, Becky and Lauren took the lift down from the Bonds' flat to Reception on Tuesday morning. Mia wasn't with them as she'd gone to the stables as usual.

Lauren nodded. 'And she's on duty again right now so we'll get a chance to ask her some questions,' she replied.

'Let's hope it was someone *completely* different from Sara who handed over the parcel,' Becky said hopefully. 'Someone short and dark-haired! That would put Sara in the clear.'

The three girls went up to the reception desk where Sophie was working on the computer.

'Sophie, could we talk to you for a minute?' Lauren murmured.

'Of course,' Sophie said with a friendly smile. 'What's up?'

Quickly Lauren explained about the dead roses and how they didn't believe Sara was involved.

'So do you remember anything about the person who dropped off the package?' Jas asked eagerly.

Sophie sighed. 'The police have asked me this already,' she said, 'and I can't remember much about it, to be honest. I was really busy with people checking in and out at the time. It was a tall, blonde woman, that's all I know.'

Jas's heart sank. 'So it *could* be Sara,' she whispered to Becky and Lauren.

'Yes, but there are lots of tall blonde women around at the moment because of London Fashion Week,' Becky pointed out. 'That description probably fits most of the models!'

'Hello, girls,' said a voice behind them.

Jas, Becky and Lauren turned to find Sara trudging towards them, having just come out of the lifts. Jas was shocked to see how ill and nervous she looked, compared to the beautiful, happy girl who'd gone off to the party just a few nights ago.

'I'm glad I've caught you,' Sara went on. 'I

wanted to say goodbye. I've decided to check out early and go home.'

'But why?' Becky asked.

'I'm too upset to work with all this stuff going on,' Sara said in a trembling voice. 'I've pulled out of all my remaining London Fashion Week shows. But I don't know *what* I'm going to do about my Princess Pink shoots. I'll have to try and carry on with those.' She bit her lip. 'If I lose that contract, I'm done for.'

'Oh, we're *so* sorry, Sara,' Jas said sympathetically.

'Thank you,' Sara answered gratefully. She glanced at Sophie. 'I'd like to check out, please,' she said. She was just asking if one of the porters could collect her bags from her room when she was interrupted by her phone ringing in her coat pocket. 'Oh, please excuse me.'

As Sara moved away to take her call, Lauren leaned over the desk to whisper to the receptionist. 'Sophie, is *that* the woman who dropped off the package?'

Sophie stared at Sara. 'I'm not sure,' she said doubtfully. 'I don't *think* so. But it *could* be.'

Sara was still on the phone, but she was staring at the girls with wide, upset eyes. What little colour had been in her face had now all drained away, leaving her as white as a ghost.

'Sara, what's the matter?' Lauren asked.

Sara covered the mouthpiece of her phone with a shaking hand. 'It's my agent, Courtney,' she said. 'She's just heard that somehow a story has been leaked to the newspapers that I'm stalking Josh Tyler!'

CHAPTER SEVEN

Jas, Lauren and Becky stared at each other in shock as Sara began speaking to her agent again in a low voice.

'This is getting worse and worse!' Lauren exclaimed. 'Do you think Josh Tyler went to the papers himself?'

'He might have done,' Becky speculated. Then an idea struck her. 'Or maybe someone else tipped them off,' she went on slowly.

'Like who?' Jas asked.

'Well, what about the person who's sending Sara those spiteful text messages?' Becky pointed out. 'Whoever it is obviously hates her. And they *must* know what's going on with Sara and Josh because Josh was mentioned in the text that Sara showed me and Lauren on the night of the party.'

'I think you're right, Becks!' Jas exclaimed. 'The person who's sending Sara the nasty texts *must* be the same person who's sending Josh the horrible emails. And they're trying to get Sara blamed for it!'

Lauren nodded. 'Yes, it definitely looks like someone's out to get Sara, doesn't it? But who?'

Becky was about to say something when Sara rang off and put her phone away.

'My agent says that there are paparazzi swarming all over my front garden back home!' Sara said forlornly, biting her lip. 'I'd be much better off staying here at the hotel.' She stared miserably at the girls. 'Someone really *is* out to hurt me, aren't they? Do you think the person who sent the texts told the papers all these lies about me? Or am I just being paranoid?'

Becky shook her head. 'That's just what we were thinking,' she replied.

'I'd better go and unpack again!' Sara forced a smile. 'Well, if I can't go home, I can't think of anywhere else I'd rather be than the Mayfair Park—' She broke off as her phone rang again. 'Excuse me.'

Becky, Jas and Lauren watched as Sara answered it.

'Hello?' Sara was silent for a moment as she listened. 'No,' she whispered at last, looking close to tears again. 'No, I don't want to make any comment at the moment.' And abruptly she ended the call.

'That was a reporter from one of the national newspapers,' Sara said with a sigh. 'They're going to be pestering me from now on.'

Right on cue her phone rang again.

'Why don't you turn it off?' Lauren suggested. 'If anyone wants to reach you, they can come through the hotel switchboard, and they'll monitor the calls for you.'

'That's a good idea.' Quickly Sara turned off her phone. 'I think I'll go back to my room. Thank you *so* much for your support, girls.'

'I wish there was something we could do to help,' Becky said to Jas and Lauren as Sara rushed off to the lifts, still looking as if she was about to cry.

'Maybe we can.' Lauren took her own phone out of the pocket of her jeans. 'I forgot to tell you that Chloe gave me her number yesterday. She asked me to keep her up to date with what's happening, so I think I ought to give her a ring. Maybe she'll come over to see Sara.'

'Yes, Sara definitely needs her friends around her at the moment,' Becky agreed. She and Jas waited in silence as Lauren called Chloe and briefly explained what had happened. Becky could tell from the responses Lauren was making that Chloe was really upset and worried about Sara and was determined to come and see her friend.

'Chloe's just finished modelling at one of the London Fashion Week shows, and she's getting a cab over here as soon as she's got changed,' Lauren reported back as she ended the call. 'Poor Chloe, she was nearly in tears when I told her what was going on. She asked us if we'd wait here in the lobby for her.'

'OK,' Becky agreed.

'We can discuss the case while we wait,' added Jas.

'Well, we haven't got very far yet, have we?' Lauren sighed, curling up on one of the large leather sofas. 'We're pretty sure that someone's out to make Sara's life a misery – but who is it?'

'Do you think it could be Josh Tyler himself?' Jas asked as she and Becky joined Lauren on the sofa. 'I can't think why he'd want to do such a thing, though!'

'What about his girlfriend, Amy?' Becky suggested. 'She might be jealous if she thinks there's something going on between Josh and Sara.'

'But Sara said herself that she and Josh were

just friends,' Lauren pointed out. 'They'd been emailing, but they hadn't seen each other since they filmed the TV ad. I don't think there was much to be jealous of, really.'

'So we're back to square one, then.' Jas frowned. 'We have to face the facts that we have NO decent suspects!'

The girls spent the next fifteen minutes going over and over everything that had happened since Sara arrived at the hotel until Becky felt her mind was in a spin. Whichever way they looked at it, Jas was right. There didn't seem to be *any* solid clues to the identity of Sara's tormentor.

As they were chatting, Becky gradually became aware of something happening outside the hotel. She looked a little closer and realized, with a sinking heart, that there were a few photographers and reporters hanging around at the bottom of the hotel steps.

'Look!' Becky groaned, pointing them out to Lauren and Jas. 'They must be here because of Sara.'

'Oh no!' Lauren exclaimed. 'Well, at least she's safe in the hotel as long as she doesn't go out. But I'd better warn Dad.'

Lauren jumped up and headed for her father's

office, with Jas and Becky close behind her. Mr Bond was just on his way out and they almost bumped into him.

'Dad, the press are outside,' Lauren told him. 'And it looks like there's more of them arriving every minute.'

'Yes, I've just had a tip-off from security,' Mr Bond said with a frown. 'Don't worry, Lauren, I'll sort it out.'

As the girls went back to their sofa, the hotel doors opened and Chloe rushed in. Becky, Jas and Lauren hurried to greet her.'

'Oh, thanks so much for calling me, and for looking after Sara, girls.' Chloe gave each of them a quick hug. 'I just can't believe what's going on at the moment. It all seems so unreal.'

'I know,' Lauren told her. 'I bet Sara'll be really glad to see you.'

'Well, I texted her to say I was coming, but she hasn't replied,' Chloe said with a frown.

'She's turned her phone off because reporters were calling her,' Becky explained.

Chloe's frown deepened. 'That lot are like vultures!' she exclaimed, glaring at the swelling ranks of paparazzi outside. More photographers and reporters had arrived during the last five minutes. 'I'd better go straight up and see her.

And you *will* let me know straightaway if anything else happens, won't you, girls?' Chloe went on anxiously. 'I'm just *so* worried about poor Sara.'

'Of course we will,' Becky promised.

Chloe flashed them a smile and dashed off to the lifts.

'Let's go and have a drink in the café-bar,' Lauren suggested to Jas and Becky. 'Sara will be OK now Chloe's with her.'

The girls wandered into the café-bar, which was almost empty, and ordered strawberry ice-cream floats from Kyle, the bar manager.

'I wonder what's going to happen next?' Jas mused, scooping up her ice-cream with a long thin spoon. 'I mean, Sara can't stay in the hotel for ever, can she?'

'No, and I think she told me she has another Princess Pink shoot this Thursday,' Lauren remembered. 'Sara must be really worried about losing the Princess Pink job with all this bad publicity going on.'

'Yes, she told us it's her biggest job, isn't it?' Becky agreed.

The girls were just finishing off their ice-cream floats when their conversation was interrupted by Charlie and Joe. They came rushing into the café-bar, skidding to a halt at the girls' table.

'The police are back!' Charlie whispered, glancing at the other guests to make sure they weren't listening.

'Why?' Lauren asked, glancing anxiously at Becky and Jas.

'I heard Dad tell Mum that they're going to take Sara down to the station for questioning!' Charlie explained.

Becky's heart lurched. 'We *have* to go and see what's happening,' she said to Jas and Lauren.

The girls jumped to their feet and hurried out of the café-bar, Charlie and Joe at their heels. But as they reached the lifts, Mrs Bond came over to them from reception.

'Where are you going?' she asked.

'To see Sara—' Lauren began.

But Mrs Bond shook her head. 'No, not this time,' she said firmly. 'You're to keep well out of the way.'

'But Sara's been getting poisonous text messages from someone!' Jas explained.

'This is a mystery, and we can help!' Becky added.

'I know all about the text messages,' Mrs Bond replied. 'Come with me, all of you.'

She led Jas, Becky and Lauren into the small hotel lounge nearby, which was empty. Charlie and Joe followed them in, and then Lauren's mum shut the door.

'Look, I know you won't want to believe this, girls,' Mrs Bond said quietly, 'but the police have investigated those text messages Sara received. And they've reached the conclusion that Sara has been sending those message to herself, via the Internet!'

CHAPTER EIGHT

There was a stunned silence. All the girls were in shock, and even Jas, who was hardly ever lost for words, couldn't get her head around what Lauren's mum had just said about Sara sending messages to her own phone from the Internet. Was that even *possible*, Jas wondered. She'd never heard of it before.

'The police think that Sara has been sending the messages to herself?' Lauren repeated in tones of disbelief. 'But that sounds really weird, Mum.'

'I told you she was suspicious from the very start!' Charlie butted in triumphantly, but Lauren ignored him.

'How did Sara *do* that, Mrs Bond?' Becky asked, looking perplexed.

'I'm not sure,' Lauren's mum replied. 'Mia could probably explain it to you. But the point is that although I know you all like Sara, and she *seems* very nice, she obviously has some serious problems. And I don't want any of you getting involved.'

'Maybe Sara has schizophrenia or something,' Becky suggested. 'She might be doing all these things and not even realizing it.'

'And that's even more reason why you girls shouldn't be involved,' Mrs Bond pointed out.

'I don't believe it!' Lauren declared. 'Sara's so lovely and she's been *so* upset about all this. And if the police can't prove it, then we have to help her!'

'Lauren—' Mrs Bond began warningly. But Lauren had already gone over to the door and opened it. Then Jas saw her freeze in the doorway.

'The police are taking Sara away!' Lauren blurted out.

Jas and Becky rushed to join her. The police were leading Sara across the lobby, with Chloe trailing along helplessly in their wake. Sara looked pale but composed, even though everyone in Reception was staring. Meanwhile, Chloe looked totally distraught.

As they watched, a tall woman with flowing blonde hair and a black-and-white checked coat strode in through the hotel doors, the high heels of her over-the-knee boots clicking loudly on the marble floor.

'Sara, *darling*!' the woman called, throwing her arms around her. 'It looks like I got here just in time.'

'Hello, Courtney,' Sara said bravely, hugging her back. The girls realized that this must be Sara's agent, Courtney Lee. 'I'm just going to the police station to answer some questions.'

'I'll send my lawyer along to look after you, just in case,' Courtney said immediately, taking out her phone.

Sara had now noticed the large crowd of press massed at the bottom of the hotel steps behind the steel barriers erected by the hotel security team. She looked really scared.

'Can't we go out the back way or something?' Sara pleaded with the policemen.

'Sorry, Miss MacDonald,' one of the officers replied. 'Our car's parked out front. And anyway, you're not under arrest.'

'There's no reason for you to hide away, Sara,' Courtney yelled encouragingly. 'Remember, there's no such thing as bad publicity!'

Jas, Becky and Lauren hurried out of the lounge, but they didn't have time to speak to

Sara before the police led her out of the hotel. They felt very sorry for Sara as the press began taking pictures and shouting questions at her.

'Are you guilty, Sara?'

'Have you been stalking Josh Tyler, Sara?'

'Have you been arrested?'

Jas, Becky and Lauren watched from the top of the stairs as Sara paused on her way down.

'No, I haven't been arrested,' she said quite steadily. 'I'm just helping the police with their enquiries because I want to find out who's responsible as much as they do.'

Sara didn't say anything more and the police officers led her over to their car. Jas, Becky and Lauren watched sadly as Sara was driven away. At least she'd been quite calm, Jas thought. The papers would have *loved* it if Sara had fallen to bits.

'Can't you do anything, Courtney?' the girls heard Chloe begging their agent.

'I'll go over to the police station myself in a little while and see how Sara's getting on,' Courtney promised, finishing her call to her lawyer. 'But first I simply *must* have a shot of caffeine to cope with all this trauma!' And she headed over to the café-bar, dragging Chloe along with her.

'Now remember what I've told you, girls,' Mrs Bond warned them. 'Sara may be charged today, or she may not, but I don't want you getting involved in this situation any further. Is that clear?'

'It's clear, Mum,' Lauren muttered.

'So that's that, then.' Becky heaved a frustrated sigh as Mrs Bond left them. 'We'll never find out who's doing all this to Sara now.'

'Actually, I didn't *promise* Mum I'd stop helping Sara,' Lauren said innocently. 'I just said it was clear she *wanted* me to.'

'Lauren Bond!' Jas exclaimed, a twinkle in her dark eyes. 'Talk about devious!'

'I just don't want to let Sara down,' Lauren replied.

'You know, it would be good to talk all this through with Mia,' Becky said thoughtfully. 'It might help clear our heads. And I bet she'd like to know what's going on.'

'We never see Mia any more these days,' Lauren moaned. 'It's just not the same without her.'

'I've got a plan for that!' Jas announced immediately.

*   *   *

'Woof! Woof! Woof!'

'Hello, Benjie,' Jas called. She, Becky and Lauren had just rung the Lopezes' doorbell, and they could hear Benjie the Labradoodle barking a welcome on the other side of the door.

'Hello, girls.' Mia's mum opened the door, holding Benjie by the collar and smiling at them. Mrs Lopez looked a lot like Mia, Jas thought – she had the same long, dark, shiny hair and big brown eyes. 'Is Mia expecting you?'

'No, we thought we'd surprise her!' Becky replied.

Mrs Lopez laughed. 'Well, she's in her room so go straight up. You know the way, don't you? But I'd better warn you, she might have dozed off. It's hard work looking after Sparky.'

Jas, Becky and Lauren stepped into the hallway and knelt down to make a fuss of Benjie who went mad with joy, licking their hands as they stroked his curly white coat. The hall was filled with coats and trainers and piles of newspapers waiting to be recycled, and there was a furry cat-bed hanging off the radiator although there was no cat inside. A big vase of red tulips stood on the telephone table next to a jumble of pens, notepads, keys and photos in silver frames. It was a bit of a mess, but it was a nice, *friendly* mess, Jas decided.

As the girls went towards the stairs, they passed the living-room. Jas glanced in and saw Marcus and Miles, Mia's older brothers, taking a computer apart. They were so engrossed in what they were doing, neither of them looked up as the girls went by. Jas grinned as she saw a big, furry brown rabbit with floppy ears lolloping around their feet.

'How many pets does Mia have now?' Lauren enquired as the three of them went upstairs.

'One dog, two cats, goldfish, four guinea-pigs and two rabbits,' Becky said promptly, knocking on Mia's bedroom door. 'Or is it three rabbits? I can't remember.'

'Come in,' Mia called from inside.

'Surprise!' Jas, Becky and Lauren said together, poking their heads around the door.

Mia was lying on her bed watching TV, her two cats Sylvester and Sasha curled up next to her. She looked a bit tired, but her face broke into a delighted smile.

'Oh, it's great to see you!' Mia exclaimed. 'Come in and sit down, if you can find a space without a cat!'

Jas, Becky and Lauren squeezed onto the bed, trying not to disturb the two black and white cats that purred sleepily as the girls stroked them.

'We've been missing you, Mia,' said Lauren. 'So we thought we'd come and say hi.'

'I know, I've been missing you too,' Mia admitted. 'I love Sparky to bits, but looking after a horse is much harder than I thought it was going to be. Especially as I've got so many of my own pets to care for!'

'How *is* Sparky?' Jas asked.

'Oh, he's lovely!' Mia said enthusiastically, 'but he's been quite naughty the last few days. He's learned how to open the latch on his stable door to get out into the yard. And not only that, he's started to let some of the other horses out of *their* stables too!'

Jas, Becky and Lauren giggled.

'Clever little Sparky!' said Becky.

'I've had to tie his stable door up with string to keep him inside,' Mia went on. 'But I bet it won't take him long to work out to get around *that*! So, how's everything going at the hotel? How's Sara?'

'Oh, we've got loads to tell you!' Jas declared, and she plunged straight into an account of everything that had happened earlier. Mia listened intently, her eyes wide.

'So the police think Sara's been sending the nasty text messages to herself?' Mia said slowly. 'But *you* don't believe it?'

'No, we don't,' said Lauren. 'But we've come to a bit of a dead end, to be honest. We don't really have any suspects.'

'You obviously need someone with brains to help,' Mia replied with a grin. 'Like me, for instance! Seriously, though, I'd love to help Sara, if she's as nice as you say, but I'm at the stables so much at the moment.'

An idea suddenly popped into Jas's head. 'I've got a plan!' she announced. 'Why don't Lauren, Becky and I take it in turns to help you out with Sparky? It'd be much quicker with two people.'

'Brilliant plan, Jas!' Lauren and Becky said together.

'That'd be great.' Mia's eyes were shining with gratitude. 'Are you sure you don't mind?'

'Course not,' Lauren replied. 'I'll come over tomorrow – and we might even get Charlie and Joe to come and help muck out Sparky some time – *if* we tell them it's essential spy training!'

The girls shrieked with laughter. Jas felt very

pleased with herself for coming up with the idea. At least the girls would be all together again, and they could continue trying to help Sara and solve the mystery of who was trying to ruin the model's career.

If only they could find a decent suspect . . .

CHAPTER NINE

'Come and meet Sparky, Lols!' Mia said, beginning to untie the string she'd looped around the stable latch to stop the horse escaping. It was the following morning, and Lauren's turn to help Mia.

'Has Sparky worked out how to undo the knot yet?' asked Lauren as they went into the stable.

'Not yet.' Mia laughed. 'But he *does* keep staring at the string, and I know he's thinking about it!'

'Hi, Sparky.' Lauren patted Sparky's white mane and the horse dipped his head down towards her. His dark eyes were particularly alert and intelligent, Lauren noticed. 'You're a *very* handsome boy, aren't you?'

Sparky gave a soft whinny, almost as if he was agreeing, which made Lauren and Mia laugh.

'I'll just put Sparky in the field out of the way.'
Mia led the horse out of the stable and over to
the field at the back of the yard. There she
opened the gate so that Sparky could trot inside
the field. 'Then we'll get on with mucking out.'

'OK,' said Lauren, pulling a face. 'I've never
got up early before to shovel horse poo, Mia, I'll
have you know!'

'Neither had I before I started looking after
Sparky!' Mia replied. 'You soon get used to it,
though, and it's really important to muck out
regularly, otherwise living in a dirty stable can
make a horse very ill.'

Lauren was very glad she'd worn her oldest
clothes as Mia showed her how they had to
shovel out all of Sparky's soiled sawdust
bedding, leaving only the clean stuff behind.
Then they added more clean sawdust on the
stone floor. It was a bit smelly, Lauren thought,
but it wasn't too bad, and besides, it was fun to
work alongside Mia and chat to her after not
seeing much of her for the last few days. As they
filled Sparky's hayrack and changed the water in
his drinking bucket, they talked a lot about Sara
and all the strange things that had been
happening since she arrived at the hotel.

'It's *so* frustrating that we're just not getting

anywhere,' Lauren told Mia as they put some pony nuts in a bucket for Sparky. 'I'm not even sure where Sara is at the moment. I asked at the Reception desk, and they said she didn't come back to the hotel last night.'

'I hope she hasn't been arrested,' Mia said anxiously.

Lauren shook her head. 'I don't think so. We'd have heard about it by now.'

When the stable was clean, they went over to the field to collect Sparky. He was cantering around the frosty grass, clearly enjoying being outside.

'What if he doesn't want to come back to his stable?' Lauren asked.

'Oh, he's well trained,' Mia replied. 'But I always have something special with me to make sure he *does* come back.'

'What's that?' Lauren asked.

Smiling, Mia took a plastic bag of apple slices from her pocket. Immediately Sparky came galloping over eagerly. Then he stopped by the gate and waited quietly to be offered the apple.

'He knows he won't get it if he's too pushy and excited!' Mia said. 'Here, you give some to him.' And she offered the bag to Lauren.

Lauren put one of the apple slices on her hand

and held it out flat. Sparky took it gently and then gobbled it up, crunching the apple with relish. Then Mia led him out of the field and back into his stable.

'Thanks, Lauren,' Mia said gratefully as they walked home together. 'It's *so* much quicker and much less hard work with two people.'

'Well, Jas, Becky and I will carry on helping you until Suzie comes back,' Lauren promised. 'Which means *you'll* have time to help *us* with our detective work.'

'Don't forget I haven't even met Sara yet,' Mia pointed out.

'You'll LOVE her!' Lauren said confidently. 'Why don't you come over to the hotel with me right now, and we can see if Sara's around?'

'OK,' Mia agreed.

As she and Mia walked back to the hotel, Lauren started wondering all over again what had happened to Sara after she'd left with the police the day before. She could ask again at the Reception desk if Sara had come by to collect her things, Lauren decided. Meanwhile, she was absolutely starving, even though she'd had cereal and toast before going over to Mia's.

'Looking after a horse is hard work, isn't it, Mia?' Lauren said with a grin. 'There's a plate of pancakes with maple syrup calling my name from the café-bar!'

'Sounds great,' Mia replied with a grin.

'I'll just ask at Reception if Sara's come back yet,' Lauren added.

Mia and Lauren hurried up the steps of the hotel and into the lobby. Lauren was about to go over to Reception to ask about Sara, when a familiar face sitting in one of the café-bar windows caught her eye. It was Sara herself.

Lauren nudged Mia. '*That's* Sara,' she said, pointing her out.

Her heart suddenly racing, Lauren led Mia into the café-bar and over to Sara, hoping her mum didn't spot her. Sara, looking very depressed, was picking at a big bowl of fruit salad, but she wasn't really eating it.

Suddenly Sara glanced up and saw Lauren and Mia. Her pale face broke into a friendly smile.

'Lauren! Come and join me.' Sara pulled out a chair for Lauren. 'I'm so glad to see you. And this must be Mia?'

Mia nodded. 'Hello,' she said, a little shyly, smiling at Sara.

'It's lovely to meet you after all this time, Mia,' Sara said. 'Lauren and the others have talked about you so much, I feel as if I know you already!'

'I was worried when you didn't come back to the hotel last night, Sara,' Lauren told her.

'Oh, I went to stay with Courtney,' Sara explained. 'My agent, you know. But the press soon got onto the fact that I was there and they all gathered outside her house. Courtney has young kids, so it wasn't really very fair on them, and I decided to come back to the hotel. Besides, all my stuff is here.' She forced a smile. 'I'm staying on in the hotel for a few more days while the press interest dies down, hopefully.'

'So what happened at the police station?' asked Mia.

'Well, they don't have enough evidence to charge me,' Sara said with a shrug. 'Honestly, the idea that I could have sent those text messages to myself from the Internet is just *ridiculous*. I'm not really techie-minded, and I wouldn't even have a clue! My ex-boyfriend used to sort out all my computer stuff for me.'

Lauren nodded. She was absolutely convinced that Sara was telling the truth. 'What's happening with all your modelling jobs? Have you cancelled them?'

Sara nodded. 'Yes, but Chloe offered to stand in for me, so I haven't really let anyone down. I was supposed to have a Princess Pink shoot tomorrow, but the company have suggested that we postpone it, considering what's going on at the moment. At least they haven't dropped me altogether, I suppose.'

'So Princess Pink are standing by you?' Lauren commented, glancing at Mia. 'That's great.'

'Yes, but for how long?' Sara toyed miserably with a pineapple slice. 'They're *such* a well-known brand, they won't want to be associated with anything dodgy. I don't know *what* I'll do if I lose that contract . . .'

'Look, now that you're back, I'm going to call Jas and Becky right away and get them to come over.' Lauren took out her phone. 'Then we can *all* put our heads together and try to figure out who could have sent those messages to your phone, *pretending* to be you in order to fool the police.'

'Thanks, Lauren,' Sara said, brightening up a little.

There was someone very cunning behind all this, Lauren reflected as she began texting the other girls. Someone who wanted to upset Sara and perhaps ruin her whole life. Lauren was determined that the Mayfair Mystery girls were going to find out exactly who that person was.

* * *

'I know you wouldn't think it to look at Mia, Sara,' Jas said teasingly, as they all gathered around the table in the café-bar a little later, 'but Mia is a total computer genius! She'll help us get to the bottom of this.'

Mia grinned. She and Lauren had been chatting to Sara for half an hour while they waited for Jas and Becky to arrive, and Mia had taken to Sara instantly. She was obviously very beautiful, but she also seemed to be a warm, genuine and generous person. Sara had insisted on ordering drinks for the girls, and had asked Mia all about how she was getting along with Sparky.

'Jas is right,' Becky put in. 'If anyone can explain all this stuff about texts from the Internet, Mia can.'

'Well, it's simple, really,' Mia said with a shrug. 'There are lots of websites where you can sign up for an account to do just that. In fact, it's so easy that someone else could have signed up, pretending to be Sara – if they knew enough of her personal details. Then, when the police investigated the account the texts were sent from, they'd think it was Sara who'd signed up.'

'OK, so who knows lots of stuff about you, Sara?' Lauren asked.

'Yes, the kind of details that are used for

signing up for accounts and for passwords or memorable words,' Becky added. 'Things like your date of birth and your mother's maiden name.'

'Or your first pet's name,' Mia put in.

'That's *actually* what I use, Mia,' Sara replied, her eyes twinkling. 'My password is always the name of my tabby kitten when I was a little girl.'

'Do you change it regularly?' Jas asked.

'Not really.' Sara pulled a face. 'I know I should, but I'm so bad at remembering passwords. It's easier just to keep the same one.'

'So who would know all your details?' Lauren said.

'Well, let me see . . .' Sara thought for a moment. 'My mum knows, and a few close friends like Chloe. Courtney, my agent, is another. Oh, and my ex-boyfriend, Rob Knowles.'

'Ex-boyfriend?' Jas repeated.

Sara nodded. 'Rob and I got on brilliantly, but he travels a lot for his job and so do I, so things got very complicated.' She sighed. 'I thought it was best to finish it.'

Mia glanced at Jas, Becky and Lauren, wondering if they were thinking the same thing as she was – that this whole situation had seemed to start when Sara had made that commercial with Josh Tyler, and they were romantically linked in the media. Was it possible that Rob was jealous and out for revenge?

'What does Rob do, Sara?' Lauren said casually.

'Oh, he's a really well-known computer games designer,' Sara replied. 'What he doesn't know about computers isn't worth mentioning! He always sorted out my PC stuff for me when we were together.' Then she frowned. 'But Rob couldn't have anything to do with all this – he's *such* a sweetie.'

Mia didn't say anything. She glanced at Jas, Becky and Lauren, and this time she was *sure* that all four of them were thinking the same thing.

Computer-whiz Rob was beginning to look like a very likely suspect!

CHAPTER TEN

'So we're all agreed then that we ought to investigate Rob Knowles?' Lauren asked, looking around at Jas, Becky and Mia.

Sara had left them a few minutes before to go up to her room, looking rather depressed as she saw the photographers and reporters beginning to lurk around the hotel steps again. Someone had obviously tipped them off that Sara was back, Lauren thought, because there hadn't been any press around when she and Mia got back from the stables earlier.

'Of course we should investigate him,' Jas said, and Mia nodded.

But Becky was frowning. 'Hang on a minute. Sophie said that the package of dead roses was handed in by a *woman*.'

'Yes, but Rob could have got a friend to do it, without telling her what the package was,' Mia pointed out.

'Oh, I didn't think of that,' Becky agreed.

'It's possible Rob's angry because Sara dumped him,' Lauren said, 'but we can't assume that's true until we've talked to him.'

'Yes, somehow we have to find out if he's over Sara, or if he's out for revenge,' Becky said.

'So we have a problem then,' Jas sighed. 'Even if we find out where Rob lives from Sara and we go to see him, we can't just turn up and interrogate him! He'll immediately want to know *why*.'

'If only we could find some other way just to meet up with him *casually*,' Becky said thoughtfully. 'Then we could lead the conversation around to Sara and watch how he reacts.'

'OK, well, our next mission is to work out exactly how we're going to approach Rob, then,' Jas said firmly.

'You sound like Charlie and Joe, talking about missions!' Lauren laughed. 'But you're right, Jas. It's going to be difficult, and we need some kind of plan . . .'

The girls stayed in the café-bar for another hour, talking things over, but didn't really get very far. Even Jas couldn't come up with any ideas. It was very frustrating, Lauren thought, as she headed back up to the Bonds' flat after the girls had gone home. Rob could be the very person they were looking for and yet there didn't seem to be any way to find out if he really *was* responsible for Sara's predicament . . .

Charlie was in the living-room, playing one of his computer games when Lauren walked in. Lauren flopped down onto the sofa, pulling a face. None of the girls were really into games, although Mia sometimes played with her brothers. Charlie, however, was fanatical about them. At the moment he was engrossed in his current favourite, which was called *Roundabout Races* and he didn't even look up when Lauren walked into the room.

As far as Lauren could see, the game seemed to involve Captain Charisma, Charlie's character, attempting to win a race by completing complicated challenges to upgrade his vehicle while the race was actually in progress. At the moment Charlie had amassed enough points for Captain Charisma to switch from a car to a jet plane, and he was now soaring along above all the other competitors on the race circuit.

'Charlie, have you ever heard of a games designer called Rob Knowles?' Lauren asked on impulse.

Charlie turned to stare at her in surprise. "Course I have!' he declared. 'He's only one of the best games designers *ever*. In fact, me and Joe are—'

There was a loud SPLAT from the TV as Captain Charisma's plane crashed into a mountain because Charlie hadn't been monitoring his progress. Charlie sighed with annoyance as the captain was now demoted to a horse and cart, trundling along slowly behind the other competitors.

'What were you going to say?' Lauren asked impatiently.

'Mum's taking me and Joe to a computer games convention on Friday,' Charlie replied, keeping his eyes on the screen this time. 'Rob Knowles is going to be there, and he'll be talking about his new game that launches later this year. Everyone says it's going to be the hottest game in the whole world!'

'Fantastic!' Lauren gasped, hardly able to believe her luck. 'Jas, Becky, Mia and I will come with you. We want to talk to Rob, *and* we've got a mission for you and Joe. You *have* to help us pretend to be games fans!'

Utterly bewildered, Charlie turned to look at her again. 'Why?'

'Oh, Rob used to be Sara's boyfriend and we're hoping he might come and see her to cheer her up,' Lauren explained quickly. She didn't want to tell Charlie the whole truth in case he let something slip in front of their mum.

Charlie was about to ask another question when Captain Charisma failed to see a secret trap set by one of the other competitors in his path. The horse, the cart and the captain fell down the hole, and the captain was now without a vehicle and had to walk around the circuit. Charlie groaned loudly.

'I'm right back at the beginning of the game!' he complained. 'OK, me and Joe will help you – but only if you take games *seriously* from now on. And you can start by being Captain Charisma's sidekick, Gloria Glamour' – he thrust a handset at Lauren – 'and win me back some points!'

'I hope we can pull this off,' Jas whispered to Becky, Mia and Lauren. It was Friday morning and they were queuing for tickets at the doors of the conference centre where the computer games convention was taking place. 'I think I might just go to pieces if anyone asks me any serious questions about computer games!'

'Well, Charlie and Joe *did* spend all day yesterday giving us a crash course in gaming,' Lauren said with a grin as the queue shuffled forward. 'I never knew there was so much to learn!'

'Neither did I,' Becky agreed.

The girls had got together at the Bonds' flat yesterday with Charlie and Joe. Lauren had suggested it so that they didn't look like complete gaming novices when they met Rob Knowles, just in case he became suspicious of them. Charlie and Joe were extremely knowledgeable, and Becky's head was still spinning with all the information the two boys had poured out in a never-ending stream. They'd spent hours playing different kinds of games too, concentrating on the ones designed by Rob Knowles so that the girls would have something to talk about when they met him.

'I'm glad Mum didn't come with us in the end,' Lauren remarked. 'Actually, I think she was quite pleased to get out of it!'

As the convention was taking place only a few streets away from the hotel, Mrs Bond had decided that it was fine for the girls and Charlie and Joe to walk there on their own. Charlie and Joe were in front of the girls in the queue, but they were incredibly excited and couldn't stand still.

'Wasn't your mum surprised that we wanted

to come to a computer games convention, Lols?'
Becky asked.

Lauren shook her head. 'I think she assumed
that it was Mia who was interested, and we
were just coming along to keep her company.'

'I do quite like playing computer games sometimes,' Mia admitted, 'but I'm nowhere near as
good as Charlie and Joe and my brothers. I'm too
busy looking after all my pets to spend much
time on them!'

They had their tickets now, and Charlie and
Joe were rushing eagerly towards the huge
double doors. Inside the massive conference hall,
the girls could see rows and rows of stands and
stalls.

'Charlie, we want to see Rob Knowles first,'
Lauren said firmly, hurrying to catch up with
the two boys. 'Then you can have a look
around.'

'OK,' Charlie agreed. 'But we want to look at
everything. And that's going to take *ages*.'

'Hours.' Joe backed him up.

'Maybe all day,' Charlie added.

'Don't push it,' Lauren warned him with a
grin. 'Now, let's find Rob Knowles.'

'There he is!' Charlie pointed to a large area of
the hall that had been set aside for special guests

who were there to sign games and chat to the crowds. A large banner hung from the ceiling that read: *Meet one of the world's top games designers right here – ROB KNOWLES!*

'Brilliant!' Jas declared, heading straight towards it through the crowds. But then her face fell as she saw the long queue at the desk where Rob was busy talking to his fans.

'I think we could be here for some time, guys,' Becky said, taking out a bag of sweets and passing them around.

'It'll be worth it to get our games signed!' Charlie declared.

The girls' progress to the top of the queue was painfully slow, but Becky could see that this was because Rob was very friendly and patient, spending a lot of time chatting to everyone ahead of them. He was tall and handsome with shoulder-length dark hair and very blue eyes. Some of the people in the queue had five or six games each that they wanted Rob to sign, but Rob's charming smile never wavered.

'We're going to be ages!' Jas moaned as a boy at the head of the queue pulled ten games out of a carrier bag and presented them to Rob for signing.

'Look at it this way, at least nobody will think

it's strange if *we* spend a lot of time talking to him too,' Becky said encouragingly.

'That's true,' Jas agreed, cheering up visibly.

At last it was their turn. Rob smiled at them as they gathered eagerly around the desk.

'Hi, everyone,' he said with a grin. 'Thanks for coming.'

'Hello, Rob,' Charlie said breathlessly, 'me and my friend Joe love your games! Don't we, Joe?'

Joe nodded, too overcome with excitement to speak.

'We *love* your games too,' Lauren said, hoping she'd got all her facts right. 'My favourite is *Alien School*. It's got fantastic graphics and a brilliant storyline.'

'Oh, mine is *Ghost Party*,' Jas declared enthusiastically. 'I love the haunted house in that, and it's so funny!'

'I like the fast gameplay and smooth-running graphics in *Fairground Fantasy*,' Mia added.

'And we're *dying* to hear all about your new game that's coming out later this year,' Becky chimed in. 'Everyone's talking about it.'

Charlie grinned at the girls. He looked quite proud that they'd learned so much in such a short time, Becky thought, amused.

'Well, it's called *Rainforest Revolution*, and I think it's going to be the most exciting thing I've ever done,' Rob explained. 'It's a great storyline, but it includes environmental issues too, which is something I feel really passionate about.'

Becky glanced sideways at the other girls. It was hard to tell from Lauren's face what she was thinking, but Mia and Jas seemed to be hanging on Rob's every word. Becky wasn't quite sure how *she* felt about him. Rob seemed lovely, but was he just too good to be true?

'That sounds fantastic,' Becky commented. 'But we were also wondering whether you'd ever consider designing a game about super-models?' She ignored loud groans from Charlie and Joe. It was time to put Rob on the spot. 'We got the idea because we've just become friends with Sara MacDonald, the Princess Pink girl!'

CHAPTER ELEVEN

As Becky mentioned Sara's name for the first time, Jas looked closely at Rob to see his reaction, and she knew that Becky, Lauren and Mia were doing exactly the same thing.

Rob's face lit up. 'You know Sara?' he exclaimed.

Lauren nodded. 'Yes, and she mentioned to us that she knew you too.'

'We used to go out together,' Rob explained. 'We split up because we spent so much time apart.' Then he sighed, looking a little upset. 'I've read in the newspapers about what's happening to Sara at the moment,' he went on. 'I'd really like to get in touch and offer her some support, but I'm not sure whether she'd want to hear from me . . .'

Rob's voice trailed away. Jas was still staring at him and she was absolutely *convinced* that Rob's emotions were genuine. Jas didn't know what Becky, Mia and Lauren thought, but she really liked him.

'Can we get our games signed?' Charlie butted in, opening his rucksack.

The girls had some games provided by Charlie in their bags too, so they handed them over to Rob to be signed.

'I was thinking of designing a computer game myself,' Mia remarked casually.

'Oh?' Rob uncapped his pen. 'What kind of story are you going for?' His blue eyes twinkled at her. 'Don't worry, I won't steal your idea!'

'Actually, I was wondering about basing it on identity theft,' Mia explained, thinking swiftly off the top of her head. 'You know, a baddie steals someone else's personal details and then pretends to be that person. But I'm not sure if it would work.'

'I think that's a great idea,' Rob replied enthusiastically. 'It's not that difficult to find out stuff about people – especially if you're friendly with them. You'd be surprised how many people give away lots of personal details, and how easy it is to guess what passwords they use on their computers!'

'Yes, we're supposed to change our passwords all the time, aren't we?' Lauren murmured.

Rob nodded. 'Absolutely! But so many people don't.'

'I was wondering about having the baddie in my game sending nasty text messages to mobile phones using the Internet,' Mia went on. 'Is that possible?'

Once again Jas stared hard at Rob, but she didn't see so much as a flicker of guilt cross his face.

'Oh, yes,' he said, 'that's really easy to do.'

'Have you ever done it yourself?' Becky asked casually.

'No, never,' Rob replied, signing one of the games with a flourish. 'But I know how it works and anyone can do it. You don't have to be a computer genius.'

Jas glanced at Mia, Becky and Lauren, wondering if they'd decided that Rob was genuine. Jas was *sure* that he was.

'It's been great to meet you,' Rob told them. Jas thought he sounded very sincere too. 'And will you give Sara my best wishes?'

'Of course we will,' Jas assured him.

As the girls said goodbye and walked off, Charlie and Joe in tow, Jas sneaked a look back at Rob over her shoulder. He looked perfectly calm and composed and was chatting animatedly to the next person in the queue.

'Well?' Lauren said as Charlie and Joe stopped to investigate a stall with lots of football games. 'What do we all think?'

'Not guilty!' Jas said promptly. 'I thought Rob was *lovely*. And it's obvious he still really cares for Sara.'

'I feel the same way,' Mia agreed. 'I was watching him all the time we were talking, and he didn't react to anything we said – except looking pleased when we mentioned Sara.'

'Yes, but that might be because he's a good actor,' Becky argued.

'I agree with Becks,' said Lauren. 'Didn't you think he was a bit *too* smooth?'

Jas and Mia shook their heads.

'Rob might just come across that way because he has to meet so many people in his job,' Mia pointed out. 'He must be used to chatting to all sorts of fans.'

'Rob's *far* too nice to be the person who's pestering Sara and Josh Tyler,' Jas said firmly.

'So we're no further forward really, are we?' sighed Becky.

'We can discuss it while we wait for Charlie and Joe to look around,' Lauren said as the two boys moved on to the next stall. 'I have a feeling we could be a *long* time!'

Three and a half hours later, Charlie and Joe were finally ready to leave, clutching the new games they'd bought. The girls had spent a lot of that time discussing Rob Knowles and if he was the guilty party or not, but none of them had changed their opinion about him. It was a bit depressing that they hadn't managed to decide one way or another, Jas reflected as they headed for the coffee bar to grab a sandwich before they left. Charlie and Joe were a little way ahead of them, deep in conversation about their new purchases.

Suddenly Lauren nudged her. 'Look, there's Rob coming out of the coffee bar,' she whispered. 'Maybe we should try to have one last word with him?'

Rob was weaving his way through the crowds back towards his desk.

'Oh, hi, girls,' he said as Lauren waved at him. 'We meet again! I've just had a break for a late lunch.'

'We – um – just wanted to say sorry for chatting away to you so long earlier.' Lauren had to think fast to come up with an excuse. '*And* for asking you all those geeky computer questions! You must get fed up with it.'

Rob laughed. 'I don't, actually. It's great to be

back in the techie world after a whole month away!'

Jas's ears pricked up when she heard that. 'Where have you been, Rob?' she asked.

'I only got back yesterday morning after spending four weeks in the Borneo rainforest,' Rob explained. 'I was in the middle of nowhere, living with orang-utans and other animals! I had no phone, no computer access, no technology of any kind.' He smiled at the memory. 'I *had* to do it to research the new game and it was a real challenge, but I'm glad to be home again, to be honest.'

Jas exchanged a meaningful glance with Becky, Lauren and Mia. That proved Rob *couldn't* be the person they were looking for, Jas thought with delight. He simply wouldn't have had the opportunity to send Sara those malicious texts from the wilds of Borneo, *or* the abusive emails to Josh Tyler!

'Rob, why don't you call Sara?' Jas suggested impulsively. 'She needs all the friends she can get right now.'

Rob looked thoughtful. 'I might just do that,' he murmured. 'Bye, girls.'

'So that's that, then.' Lauren pulled a face as they hurried to catch up with Charlie and Joe.

'We're back to not having any suspects!'

'I'm glad it's not Rob, though,' Mia said. 'But what do we do now?'

'I don't know,' Jas sighed.

Feeling rather deflated, the girls had a quick lunch and then wandered back to the hotel with Charlie and Joe. It was *so* frustrating, Jas thought. Every time they thought they were a step closer to solving the mystery, they hit a brick wall . . .

'Oh no!' Lauren groaned suddenly. 'See that news stand over there? Sara's on the front page of the paper!'

The girls hurried closer to the newspaper seller to take a look. One of the photographers had used a long lens and had managed to get a picture of Sara staring out of her hotel window. She looked very sad and depressed. The newspaper had blown the picture up so that it filled almost the whole front page, except for the big black headline which read '*GUILTY?*'

'That's horrible!' Becky exclaimed. 'Poor Sara.'

Suddenly something clicked inside Jas's head. She had an image of a woman with long blonde hair watching Sara being taken away and yelling *Remember, there's no such thing as bad publicity!*

'I've just thought of something!' Jas gasped,

sounding so excited that Mia, Becky and Lauren turned to stare at her in surprise.

'You know when Sara went with the police to be questioned?' Jas gabbled, the words tumbling out of her. 'Remember when Sara's agent arrived and told her there was no such thing as bad publicity?'

The other three nodded.

'You don't mean . . . ?' Lauren began, her eyes wide with shock.

'Yes, what if Sara has been set up by her agent, Courtney Lee?' Jas broke in. 'Just to get a whole load of publicity?'

CHAPTER TWELVE

'Do you really think Courtney Lee would do something like that, Jas?' Mia asked doubtfully. She hadn't been with the others when the agent had arrived at the hotel, so she had no idea what to think.

Jas nodded. 'Look what's happened!' she declared, pointing at the news stand. 'Sara's *everywhere* at the moment. She's in the newspapers and the gossip mags – everyone's talking about her. I bet there isn't a person in the whole country who doesn't know Sara's name by now. *And* Courtney's tall and blonde – she fits the description Sophie gave us.'

'But it doesn't make sense,' Becky said slowly, trying to puzzle things out. 'Sara works for Courtney's agency. She wouldn't want Sara to lose out on modelling work, would she?'

'No, of course not,' Lauren agreed. 'Sara makes money for Courtney, and, besides,

Courtney *definitely* wouldn't want her to lose the Princess Pink contract. It's worth a lot of money.'

'But Sara *hasn't* lost it, has she?' Jas pointed out. 'She told Lauren that Princess Pink were standing by her at the moment, despite the bad publicity. I reckon Courtney has got another trick or two up her sleeve, and, very soon, she'll make something happen so that everyone will realize Sara's innocent. So, Sara has had all this publicity *and* she keeps the Princess Pink account. Result!'

'I can see where you're coming from, Jas,' Lauren agreed.

They'd reached the hotel now and Charlie and Joe had already dashed inside, eager to play one of their new games. Mia noticed that there was still quite a crowd of reporters and photographers hanging around the bottom of the steps.

'I know Courtney was a bit loud and OTT,' said Becky, 'but she *did* seem to care about Sara. Would she really do such a thing?'

'There's only one way to find out,' Mia remarked. 'And that's to go and see Courtney and try to find out if she's up to anything. Where's the agency?'

'We looked at their website when we Googled Sara,' Lauren remembered. 'It's about half an hour's walk from here, near Beacon Park.' She rolled her eyes. 'I suppose I'd better go and ask Mum if it's OK. She's let us walk there on our own before, so she'll probably say yes.'

'You're not going to tell her we're going to the agency, are you?' Jas asked, alarmed.

'I might just forget to mention it . . .' Lauren said with a wink. 'I think detectives have to bend the truth a bit sometimes! Come and wait in the lobby while I find Mum. It's cold out here.'

As they hurried up the steps, Mia heard one of the photographers call to Lauren, 'Excuse me, miss, do you know Sara MacDonald?' Mia laughed when Lauren shot him a frosty stare and simply carried on into the hotel!

Mia, Becky and Jas made themselves comfy on one of the sofas while Lauren went in search of her mum.

'You know, the more I think about this, the more sure I am that Courtney's the baddie here!' Jas said confidently. 'It all makes sense.'

'Just like with Rob, we need an excuse to go and speak to her,' Becky remarked with a frown. 'What shall we say?'

'We could tell her that we're worried about Sara and ask if there's anything we can do to help,' Mia suggested.

Jas and Becky nodded as Lauren rushed back towards them.

'Mum's up to her eyes sorting out a huge booking for a medical conference,' Lauren said. 'So let's get out of here before she starts wondering why I asked permission for us to go to Beacon Park in February!'

The girls hurried out of the hotel and set off at a brisk pace to keep warm. Half an hour later they were standing outside a tall modern building with huge plate-glass windows. There was a sign over the automatic doors that said *Courtney Lee Model Agency* in silver letters.

'Here goes!' Jas whispered.

The girls went through the doors and into a small but very stylish lobby. There were two cream leather sofas, an amazing tropical-looking plant with exotic red flowers in one corner and a glass-topped desk for the receptionist, who looked like a model herself, Mia thought. She had jet-black hair and she wore a scarlet mini-dress and matching killer heels.

'Hello, welcome to the Courtney Lee Agency, how may I help you?' the receptionist asked, obviously wondering what the girls were doing there.

'We're friends of Sara MacDonald, and we were hoping to speak to Miss Lee about her,' Becky said politely.

The receptionist's eyes had widened slightly at the mention of Sara's name.

'Please take a seat,' she said, picking up the phone. 'I'll tell Miss Lee you're here.'

'Fingers crossed she'll speak to us,' Jas whispered as they perched on the edge of one of the sofas.

After just a few moments, the receptionist beckoned them over.

'Miss Lee has appointments all afternoon, but she can spare you a few minutes.' She pointed at a door behind her. 'Just go straight through and Miss Lee's secretary, Kellie, will meet you.'

'Thank you,' Lauren said.

The girls went through the door and all of them did a double take as they entered the huge office. It was like a different, crazy world compared to the quiet, chic and stylish lobby, Mia thought with a grin. The office was busy and noisy and full of people dressed in the very latest up-to-the-minute styles. Some were rushing around the office with clipboards while others were at their desks working at computers or talking on the phone. There were pictures of models pinned to almost every spare bit of wall space, and racks of designer clothing and boxes of shoes were stacked at one end of the huge room. There were also glossy fashion magazines lying around everywhere.

'Hi, I'm Kellie, Miss Lee's secretary.' A petite, dark-haired woman dressed all in black came over to the girls. She was smiling warmly, but Mia could see she looked a little harassed. 'We're a bit behind with everything today, but Miss Lee really wants to see you, so do you mind waiting a few minutes?'

'Of course not,' Mia said.

At that moment the girls saw Courtney pop her blonde head around the door of her office further down the room. She was wearing a deep purple velvet dress with pink patterned tights and shoes that had the highest heels the girls had ever seen.

'Nadia, have you ordered my lunch?' she asked. 'And, Layla, I need to speak to *Vogue* about the fashion shoot.' Her sharp eyes roamed around the room and fixed on Kellie and the girls. 'Ah, there you are!' Courtney called. 'I won't keep you long, girls, I promise. But I just have one teeny-tiny letter to dictate to Kellie before I see you. Do take a seat.'

Kellie showed the girls over to some chairs and then scuttled off.

'So *that's* Courtney Lee!' Mia murmured. 'I see what you meant about her being OTT!'

The girls began flicking through some fashion magazines, but it was barely five minutes later before Kellie came back to collect them and usher them into Courtney's office. Mia glanced around the room as she went in. It was luxuriously furnished with a big antique mahogany desk, plush green sofas and big vases of flower arrangements, but there was something *wrong* . . . Mia frowned, trying to work out what it was.

'Thanks for seeing us, Miss Lee,' Jas said.

'Oh, do call me Courtney, my dears!' She indicated for the girls to sit down. 'Any friend of Sara's is a friend of mine.' She smiled widely at them, showing off sparkling white teeth. 'I have to say, I thought you might be newspaper reporters pretending to be Sara's friends to try and get a quote or two out of me!'

'Well, we *are* a bit young for that,' Becky said with a smile.

'And far too sweet and nice, I'm sure, to do something so devious, anyway,' Courtney added. 'The media are really *terrible* when they get so much as a hint of a story like this – they're like vultures!'

'That's what Chloe said,' Jas remarked. 'She's one of your models too, Courtney, isn't she?'

Courtney nodded. 'Yes, I took them both on while they were still at school. Chloe's an excellent model, but Sara really is something special.'

Mia was actually warming to Courtney. The agent was a larger than life character, but she seemed open and honest and straightforward. Could she *really* be the person who was making Sara's life a misery?

'Now, what can I do for you?' Courtney asked, sitting down at her desk. Looking at her, Mia once again experienced the feeling that something about this office was very, very wrong. But she still couldn't figure out what it was.

'Well, it's more what *we* can do for Sara,' Lauren replied. 'We were hoping you might be able to suggest some way we could help.'

'How lovely of you!' Courtney exclaimed. 'Well, it would be fabulous if you could ring and update me regularly on how Sara's getting on. Here's my number.' She handed Lauren a glossy business card. 'I'm trying to visit her as much as possible, but I have other clients to look after, of course.'

'We'll keep an eye on Sara,' Lauren promised.

'Perfect!' Courtney approved. 'Let's all hope this horrible situation gets sorted out very soon. Don't say anything to Sara, but I'm very afraid that Princess Pink are going to cancel her contract.' She heaved a sigh and hit a buzzer on her desk to call her secretary. 'Thanks for coming, girls. Kellie will show you out. Sorry to rush off, but I have to be in Kensington by five o'clock.'

As Courtney stood up, Mia suddenly realized what had been bugging her about the agent's office. Courtney didn't have a computer on her desk!

'I'm hoping to go and see Sara tonight,' Courtney went on as Kellie came in, 'but just in case I can't make it, I think I'll send her some flowers.' She turned to Kellie. 'Can you order a big bouquet on Goggle or whatever you call it?' Courtney asked.

Goggle?! Mia froze to the spot, hardly able to believe her ears. She just about stopped herself from correcting Courtney by yelling *It's Google, actually!* Now Mia understood exactly why

Courtney didn't have a computer on her desk. She had absolutely no idea how to use one!

'Let's get out of here,' Becky whispered as Mia stared at Courtney in absolute horror. 'And I think we're going to have to drag Mia with us because she's so shocked, she's forgotten how to walk!'

CHAPTER THIRTEEN

'Can you believe it?' Mia groaned as they left the agency. Jas could tell she was still reeling in disbelief. 'I mean – *Goggle*!'

'Well, at least we can forget Courtney as a suspect,' Lauren pointed out. 'I don't think she'd know how to turn a computer on, never mind send messages to a mobile phone.'

'So what now?' Jas wanted to know as they walked back to the hotel. 'We're doing a great job of eliminating suspects, but that means we still don't have anyone in the frame!'

'I have to go.' Mia glanced at her watch. 'I need to get to the stables to take Sparky out and feed and groom him.'

'And it's my turn to help you,' Becky added. She glanced at Jas and Lauren. 'Let us know if anything happens while we're gone, won't you?'

Jas and Lauren nodded. When they reached

the hotel, Mia and Becky hurried off, and Jas and Lauren went up the steps into Reception.

'Shall we have a sauna to warm up?' Lauren suggested. It was just starting to get dark, and it was feeling much colder.

'Sounds good,' Jas agreed.

When Lauren and Jas headed over to the lifts, they saw Chloe standing waiting too.

'Hi, Chloe,' Lauren said, 'are you going up to see Sara?'

'Hello, girls.' Chloe smiled a little wearily at them. 'Yes, I am. I've been working all day, covering a fashion shoot for Sara. But I don't want to leave her on her own too much at the moment. I think she's going stir-crazy staring at those four walls all day!'

'Can we come and say hello too?' Lauren asked.

'Oh, please do!' Chloe said, looking rather relieved. 'It's so difficult trying to cheer Sara up at the moment. She's really down. Not that I blame her one bit.'

'It's a shame you can't take Sara for a girls' night out, Chloe,' Jas suggested as they got into the lift. 'It might do her good.'

Chloe sighed deeply. 'I know, but how would we get past the paparazzi?' she pointed out. 'If they saw Sara coming out, they'd just follow her to whatever restaurant or club we were going to, and she wouldn't be able to relax at all.'

Jas turned to Lauren. 'Couldn't Sara sneak out of the back of the hotel?'

Lauren shook her head. 'There's bound to be a photographer or two hanging around there in the evenings just in case Sara decides to try and leave,' she replied. 'That's happened in the past when we've had other celebrities staying. We can't risk it.'

'Well, there must be *something* we can do,' Jas declared as the lift arrived at the second floor.

The lift doors opened. Jas, Lauren and Chloe came out – and stopped short in surprise. There was no one else around, but the three girls could see a large silver trolley, the kind used to deliver room service, moving slowly down the corridor, seemingly of its own free will.

'What's going on?' Lauren gasped.

The sound of running footsteps made them all turn round. The next second Joe came charging around the corner of the corridor, red in the face. He skidded to a halt when he saw Chloe, though.

'What *are* you up to, Joe?' asked Jas.

'I'm looking for Secret Agent Bond!' Joe whispered. 'I know he came this way!'

Lauren and Jas both realized what was happening at the very same moment. They grinned at each other and then glanced down the corridor at the trolley. It had stopped moving now. Jas guessed that Charlie was hidden under the long white tablecloth, crouched down between the trolley and the wall, and he was moving the trolley as he sneaked along the corridor.

'I suppose he could be around here *somewhere*,' Jas said casually.

Just then Joe spotted the trolley beginning to move again. He let out a gasp, raced down the corridor and whipped the tablecloth off it. Charlie was hiding between the trolley and the wall, just as Jas had guessed.

'I've found you at last, Mr Bond!' Joe said, trying to grab Charlie. 'And now you are my prisoner!'

'No way!' Charlie leaped up and dashed off down the corridor, with Joe in hot pursuit.

Lauren laughed. 'Sorry, Chloe,' she said. 'Those two are a right pair of pests.'

'Don't worry about it,' Chloe replied. 'I've got younger brothers myself!'

Jas was staring at the trolley in silence, her

brain suddenly working overtime. The trolley Charlie had been using was empty, but there was a broad metal shelf at the bottom suitable for stacking lots of plates. And it looked big enough for someone to sit on . . .

'Lauren, I've just had an idea,' Jas said excitedly. 'Quick, grab that trolley!'

Lauren looked puzzled, but at that moment the lift doors opened and Mrs Stoop, the housekeeper, came out. She clicked her tongue in annoyance when she saw the abandoned trolley. Marching over to it, she wheeled it straight over to the service lift.

'Oh, no, The Snoop's taking the trolley back to the kitchens,' Jas groaned as Mrs Stoop and the trolley disappeared into the lift. 'And I need it for my plan!'

'What plan?' asked Chloe.

'My plan to get Sara out of the hotel!' Jas replied. 'It was Charlie who gave me the idea. The bottom shelf's big enough for Sara to sit on, and we could cover it with the tablecloth and no one would be able to see her.'

'That's fantastic, Jas!' Lauren said admiringly.

'I know,' Jas agreed with a grin.

'It's a great idea, but now we don't have a trolley!' Chloe pointed out.

'Jas and I will get another one from the kitchens,' Lauren told her. 'You go and tell Sara to get dressed up as fast as she can.'

Chloe nodded and hurried off to Sara's room. Meanwhile, Jas and Lauren ran over to the service lift and pressed the call button.

'I hope The Snoop isn't hanging around by the kitchens,' Jas said anxiously.

The service lift went down and stopped at the back of the kitchens. The doors opened and both Jas and Lauren almost jumped out of their skins.

'I can hear The Snoop's voice!' Jas whispered.

Lauren peered cautiously out of the lift and then nudged Jas. 'Look, there's the trolley!'

Mrs Stoop had left the trolley just outside the lift doors. She was now standing near the kitchens, talking to two of the waitresses.

'. . . and I just found an abandoned room service trolley on the second floor!' Mrs Stoop was saying in a severe tone. 'That's just not acceptable!'

Silently Lauren and Jas tiptoed out of the lift and then wheeled the trolley inside. Neither The Snoop nor the maids noticed them. Only when the lift was safely on its way back to the second floor did Jas and Lauren burst out laughing.

'I'd love to see The Snoop's face when she sees that the trolley's vanished!' Jas giggled.

When the lift stopped, the girls wheeled the trolley out and down the corridor to Sara's room. Lauren tapped on the door and Sara opened it. She was ready to leave, wearing a pink silk dress with her hair piled up on top of her head.

'Chloe's told me all about your plan,' Sara laughed, opening the door wider so that Jas and Lauren could roll the trolley inside. Jas could see that Sara looked happier than she had since everything had gone wrong for her.

Jas bowed and lifted up the tablecloth. 'Your carriage awaits!' she announced.

Smiling, Sara picked up her pale pink heels in one hand and tucked her clutch bag under her arm. Then she climbed onto the metal shelf at the bottom of the trolley, wedging herself in.

'Are you OK?' Chloe asked anxiously.

'Fine,' Sara replied, holding firmly onto the sides of the trolley. 'Let's go!'

Lauren swung the tablecloth down so that Sara was hidden from view. Then they left the room, pushing the trolley carefully so that they didn't shake Sara around too much.

'We'll have to take the service lift,' Jas told

Chloe. 'Maybe you'd better go down in the guest lifts and we'll meet you outside?'

'Good idea,' Chloe agreed. 'The press know I'm Sara's friend, and they might get suspicious if they see the three of us with this trolley! I'll grab a taxi just around the corner and be waiting for you.'

Chloe's lift arrived first and she stepped in, whispering *Good luck!* to Sara as she did so. The service lift arrived a moment or two later, and Jas and Lauren wheeled Sara and the trolley inside.

'I hope we don't meet The Snoop anywhere!' Lauren said.

But luckily when the girls arrived on the ground floor, there was no one to be seen. Quickly Jas and Lauren pushed the trolley towards the outside doors, the hotel's service entrance where deliveries were made.

'Here goes!' Jas murmured, pulling open the door. 'Ready, Sara?'

'Ready!' came back the muffled reply.

The girls manoeuvred the trolley outside. The service entrance was at the side of the hotel, not far from the main doors and, trying to look innocent, Jas and Lauren pushed the trolley past the waiting press pack towards the taxi rank. Nobody took any notice of them, though.

Chloe was waiting in a taxi, waving at them. Jas and Lauren brought the trolley to a halt and Lauren flipped up the tablecloth.

'We made it!' she told Sara with a grin.

'Thank you so much.' Sara gave them both a quick hug and then jumped into the taxi beside Chloe.

Jas turned to Lauren as the taxi sped off. 'Mission accomplished!' she declared.

CHAPTER FOURTEEN

Yawning, Lauren glanced at her watch as she took the lift down to Reception. It was early the following morning and it was her turn to go to Mia's again. She was running a little late because she'd overslept.

Lauren stepped out of the lift and, to her delight, she saw Sara and Chloe come out of the lift next door.

'Hi.' Lauren beamed at them. 'Did you have a good night?'

'The best!' Sara said with a wide smile, looking happier than ever. 'Chloe stayed over with me after we got back, and now we're just off to the spa for a bit of girlie pampering.'

'That's great,' said Lauren.

'But I haven't told you the most important thing that's happened, yet,' Sara went on, still smiling from ear to ear. 'I received another of those horrible text messages last night while I was out!'

Lauren stared at her in confusion. 'But why do you look so happy about it?'

'Because now the police *have* to believe me when I tell them that I haven't been sending the messages to myself!' Sara explained, her eyes shining with relief. 'Chloe and I went to a club, and I wasn't anywhere near a computer last night, so that finally proves I'm innocent. I'm so relieved.'

'Me too.' Lauren gave Sara a hug. It was great to see her looking so positive and upbeat.

'Sara, aren't those the policemen who took you away to be questioned?' Chloe said, pointing at the doors.

Lauren turned and saw the two policemen coming across the lobby towards them. Their faces were grave.

'Miss Sara MacDonald, you're under arrest for harassment,' one of the policemen said sternly.

Lauren and Chloe both gasped in shock. But Sara just stood there frozen to the spot, unable to speak and looking utterly bewildered.

'You do not have to say anything, but it may harm your defence if you do not mention now or when questioned, something which you later rely on in court . . .' the policeman went on, giving Sara the official caution.

'What *is* this all about?' Chloe cried angrily. 'Has Josh Tyler had some more abusive emails then? He *must* have, or you wouldn't be arresting Sara!'

'We can't discuss any details of this case with you, miss,' the other policeman replied, handcuffs at the ready.

'Please don't,' Sara pleaded with a shudder as she glanced at the handcuffs. 'I won't be any trouble.' She turned to Lauren and Chloe. 'This is just a terrible mistake,' Sara murmured faintly. 'I'll explain about the text messages and that I couldn't have sent the one last night. Then the police will understand that someone's setting me up!'

Lauren could hardly believe her eyes as the two policemen led Sara away, one on each side of her. Everyone in the lobby, guests and staff, including Lauren's parents, were staring. Then, as the police officers led Sara down the hotel steps, cameras clicked and the reporters started yelling questions. Sara looked absolutely wretched as she was put in the police car and driven away, Lauren thought, feeling very miserable herself.

'Surely the police will believe now that Sara hasn't been sending those messages to herself,'

Lauren said to Chloe. 'And if they do, it means that someone is definitely out to get Sara – and that *must* be the same person who's sending Josh Tyler the nasty emails.'

Chloe sighed. 'Lauren, I couldn't say anything in front of Sara, but she *won't* be able to prove that anyone else is involved. There's a late-night Internet café just two doors down from the club we went to last night . . .'

'You're not saying Sara slipped out of the club, went to the Internet café and sent the text message to herself?' Lauren exclaimed, dismayed. 'You'd have noticed.'

'Well, Sara disappeared for about half an hour, that's the problem.' Chloe looked worried. 'When I found her again, she said she'd met an old friend near the bar and she was chatting to her for ages, but I was looking for her all over the club and I didn't see her . . .'

Quickly Lauren took out her phone. Things were looking really bad for Sara. She had to tell the others what had happened so that they could get together and discuss what to do next. They were Sara's only hope!

'Poor Sara.' Jas trundled the wheelbarrow full of soiled bedding out of the stable. The girls had just finished mucking out Sparky, and now they were about to groom him. 'I feel so helpless. What can we *do*?'

Lauren had sent text messages to Becky and Jas, describing Sara's arrest and suggesting that they all meet up at the stables so that they could discuss it. The other girls had been horrified to hear all the details.

'There doesn't seem to be anything we *can* do,' Becky sighed as they went over to Sparky. Mia had tied the horse to a ring on a post in the stable yard, and he was waiting patiently for them. 'We've run out of suspects, remember?'

'Here.' Mia handed Jas and Lauren some brushes. 'You can brush Sparky's tail and mane. Just be careful not to stand where he can accidentally kick you! Becky and I will use the curry combs and some stiff brushes to get all the dirt out of his coat.'

The girls were silent for a few moments as they concentrated on grooming Sparky.

'You know what I find *really* strange?' Jas frowned. 'Why on earth did Chloe tell Lauren about the Internet café?'

'Yes, it's odd, isn't it?' Mia agreed. 'If Chloe wanted to protect Sara, she could have kept quiet. Do you think she's going to tell the police that Sara might still have sent the message to herself from the café?'

Lauren looked startled. 'I don't know. Chloe didn't say.'

'Jas is right,' Becky joined in. 'Chloe went out of her way to tell you that Sara could still be guilty, Lauren. That doesn't sound to me like the kind of thing a best friend should do. Maybe Chloe secretly doesn't want to protect Sara at all?'

The girls were silent for a moment as they continued grooming Sparky.

'Maybe we should look at this in a slightly different way,' Mia remarked at last. 'Why would someone do this to Sara? What are they getting out of it?'

'You mean, who's doing well out of Sara's career going downhill?' Jas asked.

'Well, *Chloe* is, isn't she?' Becky said slowly. 'Because she's picking up all of Sara's jobs!'

'*Chloe?*' Jas gasped, her eyes wide with shock. 'But she's not a suspect – she's Sara's best friend!'

'Yes, she is – and *that* means she'd know all Sara's personal details and her computer passwords!' Lauren pointed out.

'And Chloe is tall and blonde,' Becky said.

'She could easily be the person who delivered the package of dead roses to Reception.'

All four girls stopped brushing Sparky and stared at each other with dawning excitement.

'Girls,' Jas declared, 'I think we just found ourselves a new suspect!'

CHAPTER FIFTEEN

'How *could* Chloe do this to Sara?' Lauren demanded indignantly. She was so furious, she could hardly speak. 'Some friend *she* is!'

'We don't actually know yet if it's definitely her,' Becky pointed out. 'But everything fits, doesn't it?'

'And we have yet another problem,' Jas broke in. 'Now that Sara's been arrested, Chloe isn't going to send any more text messages to Sara or any more nasty emails to Josh Tyler, is she? Not now she's got what she wanted.'

'So how on earth are we going to prove that Sara is innocent?' asked Mia.

None of the girls had any ideas. They fell silent once more, concentrating on grooming Sparky while they thought hard. Lauren was absolutely *determined* to think of a way to unmask Chloe as the real villain of the piece. But how?

As Lauren continued to brush Sparky's mane, she suddenly felt something tickling her ear. With a shriek of surprise, she spun round and found a black horse nuzzling her hair curiously.

'Mia, where's that horse come from?' Lauren asked as the horse began to wander off across the yard. 'Shouldn't he be in his stable?'

'Hey, look, it's not the only one who's escaped!' Jas said. A small white pony was also loose and trotting around, and so was a chestnut-coloured horse.

'They shouldn't be wandering around like this,' Mia cried. 'We *have* to round them up!'

Jas, Becky and Lauren hurried over to help Mia. The horses were quite docile and allowed the girls to guide them gently and quietly back into their stables.

'So how did they all get out?' Becky asked, closing the door behind the white pony.

'Well, it can't have been Sparky who freed them,' Mia pointed out. 'We've been grooming him the whole time. He hasn't been out of our sight once.'

Suddenly Lauren spotted the latch on the black horse's stable door being lifted up from the inside. A moment later the black horse trotted out into the yard again.

'There's your culprit, Mia!' Lauren laughed as Mia led the horse back into his stable. 'He must have learned how to open the door from Sparky, and then he let the other two out as well!'

'I think I'd better tie up *all* the stable doors from now on,' Mia said, shaking her head. 'Just in case any of the others have learned the same trick!'

An excited yelp from Jas at this point made them all jump. 'Oh, that's just given me an idea about Sara!' Jas exclaimed. The others stared at her, puzzled. 'Chloe isn't going to send any more nasty emails to Josh Tyler now that Sara's in police custody, because that would prove that Sara is innocent.' Jas took a deep breath. 'But what if Chloe *thought* Sara had been released and that she'd gone back to the hotel?'

'What, and it wasn't really true, you mean?' asked Becky.

Jas nodded. 'If Chloe *thought* Sara had been freed, then she'd want to incriminate Sara yet again, wouldn't she? Probably by sending another one of those abusive emails to Josh Tyler. And if we could catch her in the act . . .'

'Then the police would know that it *couldn't* be Sara because she's right there in the police station under their noses,' Lauren agreed. 'Just as *we* realized that it couldn't be Sparky who let those horses out because we were with him the whole time!'

Becky was thinking hard. 'If Chloe thinks Sara has been freed and is back at the hotel, then she'd have to send the email to Josh from Sara's laptop or from the hotel's computer room. Just to make sure the police believe it's Sara up to her old tricks again.'

'I think the police probably still have Sara's laptop for evidence,' Jas pointed out. 'I reckon Chloe would dash over to the hotel and use one of *their* computers.'

'And maybe we should add something else too, just to make Chloe feel she has to act fast,' Mia said eagerly. 'I was thinking we could tell her that Princess Pink are going to drop Sara from their advertising campaign if there's any more bad press.'

'That's another brilliant idea.' Becky patted Mia on the back. 'So what's our next move?'

'We'll go back to the hotel when we've finished grooming Sparky and I'll ring Chloe,' Lauren decided. 'We'll set the trap for her and see what she does next . . .'

'Oh, hi, Chloe,' Lauren said, hoping she sounded quite normal. Jas, Becky and Mia were sitting next to her on one of the sofas in the hotel lobby, looking nervous and excited all at the same time. 'How are you?'

'Fine,' Chloe replied. 'Well, obviously I'm still very worried about Sara.'

I think you're lying, Lauren thought. She was furious on poor Sara's behalf, but that wouldn't help Sara now. Lauren knew she had to keep calm and composed.

'I've got a day off work today, so I thought I'd go over to the police station and visit Sara,' Chloe went on.

'Well, that's why I'm ringing,' Lauren said. 'I thought you'd like to know that Sara's been released by the police! Isn't that fantastic news?'

'What?' Chloe gasped, obviously taken by surprise.

'I said, Sara's been released,' Lauren repeated, raising her eyebrows at the others. 'I knew you'd be pleased!'

'Yes, of course I am,' Chloe said hurriedly. 'Where is she now?'

'She's lying low here in the hotel,' Lauren replied. 'Courtney says if there's any more bad publicity, then Princess Pink will drop Sara from their advertising campaign.'

'Really?' Chloe sighed. 'Well, let's hope that

doesn't happen. I'll pop over to the hotel and see her as soon as I can.'

'You do that,' Lauren said. 'Bye, Chloe.' She rang off and grinned at the others. 'Well, that's that!' Lauren went on. 'I bet Chloe's on her way here right now to use the computer!'

'So what do *we* do?' Becky asked.

'We'll hide here in the lobby and wait for Chloe to turn up,' Lauren replied. 'And I've got a secret mission in mind for Charlie and Joe, which will help us catch Chloe in the act!'

CHAPTER SIXTEEN

'So you want us to go and see the security guards and make sure the CCTV cameras are covering the computer room all day,' Charlie said, staring at Lauren in bewilderment. 'Why?'

'We think Sara's best friend Chloe has set Sara up,' Lauren explained quickly. She was keeping an eye on the main doors in case Chloe suddenly arrived.

'So we pretended that Sara's been released,' Mia told the boys. 'Now we think that Chloe's going to come to the hotel and send another horrible email to Josh Tyler, hoping the police will think it's Sara again.'

'And we need proof that it's *really* Chloe,' Jas added. 'That's where the CCTV comes in – we'll have it all on film!'

Charlie and Joe looked excited.

'We won't let you down,' Joe said solemnly. 'Come on, Agent Bond!' And the two of them rushed off to the hotel's security department.

'Let's hope Chloe shows up after all our complicated plans,' Jas fretted as the four of them went over to a sofa tucked away in a quiet corner.

'She will,' Lauren said confidently, secretly hoping that she was right.

For half an hour the girls sat and waited, full of anticipation. Another half an hour passed and Lauren was almost about to give up hope when a familiar figure slipped in through a side door on the far side of the lobby.

'There's Chloe!' Lauren whispered to Mia, Becky and Jas.

Chloe was dressed all in black and her blonde hair was bundled out of sight under a grey knitted hat. She also wore huge dark sunglasses that hid most of her face. But Lauren was sure it was her. She was even more sure when Chloe made her way quietly and unobtrusively over to the computer room. As Lauren, Jas, Becky and Mia watched, Chloe went inside and closed the door behind her.

'We were totally right, then,' Becky said triumphantly. 'It was Chloe all along!'

'She's got some nerve, hasn't she?' Lauren muttered. She was furious with Chloe and felt like rushing over to confront her right away, face to face. 'Coming to the hotel like this and trying to get Sara into trouble again!'

Mia pulled a face. 'With friends like her, who needs enemies?'

The girls waited for a while, their eyes fixed on the closed door of the computer room.

'How long has Chloe been in there?' Mia asked.

'About ten minutes,' Lauren replied, checking her watch. 'She must be sending a really *horrible* email to Josh Tyler.'

'I hope Charlie and Joe are on the case,' Jas said anxiously.

'Ah, there you are, girls. Can someone *please* tell me what's going on?'

Lauren, Becky, Mia and Jas almost jumped out of their skins at the sound of a voice behind them. They turned and saw Lauren's dad staring questioningly at them.

'I've just had a call from Security,' Mr Bond went on. 'The guys on duty tonight say Charlie and Joe are dancing around the CCTV room yelling that Sara MacDonald is innocent and they've got the real culprit caught on film!'

Lauren's face lit up. 'It worked!' she exclaimed triumphantly to the others.

'Now,' said Mr Bond, 'I think someone had better tell me *exactly* what's been happening . . .'

Quickly Lauren poured out the whole story with Jas, Mia and Becky adding any bits Lauren missed out. When they'd finished, Mr Bond looked rather grave.

'This sounds serious,' he said. 'I'll have to call the police immediately.'

Jas heaved a huge sigh of relief as Lauren's dad hurried back to his office. 'Charlie and Joe must have recognized Chloe too,' she said. 'I thought maybe they wouldn't realize who she was under that disguise!'

Suddenly Lauren sat up straight. 'Here's Chloe again now!' she whispered.

Chloe had sidled out of the computer room as silently as possible and was making her way over to the exit.

'We've got to keep her here until the police arrive!' Jas said in a low voice.

The girls jumped off the sofa and hurried across the lobby.

'Chloe!' Becky called.

Chloe jumped a mile in the air. She spun round, smiling nervously when she saw Becky, Jas, Mia and Lauren close behind her.

'Oh, hi, girls,' Chloe said, trying to sound casual and relaxed.

'We nearly didn't recognize you,' Jas said innocently. 'You almost look like you're in disguise!'

'Don't be silly!' Chloe said sharply. Then, realizing how she'd sounded, she forced a smile. 'I thought the press might be hanging around again and I didn't want them to spot me.' She frowned. 'It's funny there aren't any photographers here if Sara's back.'

'I'm not sure if many people know yet that Sara's been released,' Lauren said, thinking fast.

'Are you here to see Sara, Chloe?' asked Becky.

'Of course,' Chloe replied.

'So why were you on your way out?' Becky wanted to know.

Chloe looked incredibly guilty just for a split second. 'Oh, I went upstairs and tapped on her door, but she didn't open it. I've been trying to ring her mobile too, but I'm not getting any answer.'

Lauren flashed a relieved glance at Mia, Becky and Jas. It was lucky that Sara wasn't allowed to have her mobile with her while she was in police custody!

'I think Sara said she was popping out to see Courtney,' Lauren remarked casually. 'I don't think she'll be long. Why don't you wait for her?'

'Yes, you must be dying to see her and give her a big hug!' said Jas. 'We could hang out with you while you're waiting.'

'Why don't we all go and have a drink in the café-bar?' Becky suggested.

'OK,' Chloe agreed. She looked a bit reluctant, but obviously didn't feel she could refuse without it looking like she didn't want to meet Sara.

Lauren led the way to a table and they all sat down and ordered drinks. Lauren could see Mia, Becky and Jas glancing anxiously outside the hotel every few seconds, looking for the police. She felt really on edge herself and it was a big effort to be nice to Chloe, knowing how she'd tried to ruin Sara's life.

'I don't think we've met before, have we?' Chloe sipped her coffee and glanced at Mia.

Mia shook her head. 'I'm Mia,' she said. 'Becky, Jas and Lauren are my best friends. Just like you and Sara.'

Chloe forced another smile. 'There's nothing like having good friends, is there?'

No, and you're NOTHING like a good friend!
Lauren thought to herself.

Suddenly, to her intense relief, Lauren saw a police car pull up outside the hotel. The two officers who'd arrested Sara climbed out and made their way inside. Mr Bond came out of his office to meet them and all three headed over to the café-bar.

Chloe was checking her watch. 'I think I'd better go. I'll come back to see Sara later . . .' Her voice faltered and died away as the policemen came up to her.

'Miss Chloe Price?' one of them asked sternly.

Chloe nodded, swallowing hard.

'We'd like you to come down to the station with us to answer a few questions,' the officer went on. 'We have reason to believe that you may have some information that will help with our enquiries.'

Chloe stared at them in stunned silence. 'What do you mean?' she gasped. 'You said Sara had *already* been released!'

'Did I?' Lauren shrugged. 'Well, I must have made a mistake!'

'I'm not going with you!' Chloe yelled, jumping up from her chair and backing away from the officers. 'I've got nothing to say!'

'You don't need to say anything,' Jas told her. 'It's all on the computer room's CCTV!'

Chloe turned pale as the reality of the situation hit her. Struggling for composure, she scowled at the girls. 'If you knew what I've had to put up with over the years!' she burst out loudly, her pretty face full of fury and hatred. 'It was always Sara this, Sara that, isn't Sara wonderful! She was supposed to be my friend, but I was always in her shadow. It's just not fair!' Chloe's voice rose higher. 'Sara always got everything – the nicest boyfriends, the best modelling jobs like Princess Pink – and I got NOTHING!'

'Come along, Miss Price,' said one of the policemen firmly. Lauren, Jas, Becky and Mia watched as they led Chloe out of the café-bar, accompanied by Mr Bond. A moment or two later, Chloe was in the back of the police car and it sped off.

'I can't believe it!' Jas exclaimed. The girls flung their arms around each other and jumped up and down with delight. 'Chloe's been caught, and Sara's going to be released!'

'The Mayfair Mysteries girls have done it again!' Mia sounded very proud.

'We helped, don't forget!' Charlie and Joe had

appeared in the café-bar just in time to hear Mia's comment.

'That's true, we couldn't have done it without you,' Mia agreed.

'Don't hug us!' Charlie said, alarmed.

'We were worried you wouldn't recognize Chloe,' Lauren said to the boys.

'Are you kidding?' Charlie gave a snort of disgust. 'Her disguise was rubbish – it wouldn't have fooled *anybody*.'

'She wasn't a master of disguise like me and Charlie!' Joe added.

The girls laughed. Sara would be released some time very soon, Lauren thought happily. She couldn't wait to see her again!

'Here's Sara!' Lauren called excitedly. It was later that day. She, Jas, Becky and Mia had just got out of the pool and were on their way across the lobby to the café-bar for a snack. They were all thrilled to see Sara running up the steps towards them.

'Girls, what can I say?' Sara rushed across the lobby to hug them all. 'I'm free, and it's all thanks to you! The police told me about your plan to trap Chloe, and about the CCTV. I'm just *so* grateful.'

'It must have been a real shock when you

found out it was Chloe who was behind it all,' Mia said sympathetically.

Sara's face fell. 'Oh, it was,' she admitted. 'I still can't quite believe it. It's a horrible feeling knowing that she must have hated me for *years*. I didn't have a clue. I thought we were the best of friends.'

'Chloe's a great actress!' Jas observed. 'She fooled everybody, not just you, Sara.'

'I know.' Sara nodded. 'It'll take me a while to get over this, but I'm just *so* glad I can get on with *my* life now. I thought everything was over for me when I was arrested.'

'So what happens now?' asked Becky.

'Well, Chloe's going to be charged with harassing me *and* Josh Tyler, I think,' Sara replied. 'And Courtney's told me that she's already getting huge offers from magazines like *HELLO!* to tell all about me and Chloe! And I really want everyone to know my side of the story.'

'Will you be able to make up with Josh?' Lauren wanted to know.

Sara smiled. 'We already have! I got my phone back from the police when I was released and Josh rang me just before I got back to the hotel. We're going to get together soon so I can meet his girlfriend.'

'So everything's back to normal for you,' Jas said with satisfaction. 'That's great, Sara.'

'Actually, there's something else.' Looking rather shy, Sara began to blush. 'You remember I mentioned my ex-boyfriend, Rob Knowles, the computer designer? Well, he left a message on my phone, and I called him back just now. We're going on a date next week!'

Lauren, Becky, Mia and Jas exchanged delighted glances. At that very moment Sara's phone went off, indicating that she had a text.

'It's wonderful not being frightened and upset every time I get a message!' Sara beamed, scanning the display screen. 'It's from Courtney. She's coming to pick me up and take me home, so I have to run and get my packing done. But I'll *never* forget what you've done for me, girls, and I'd *love* you to come and be special guests at one of my catwalk fashion shows some time. Will you?'

Becky beamed at her. 'Of course we will!'

After another round of hugs, Sara dashed for the lifts, humming happily under her breath.

Smiling, Lauren turned to the others.

'I hope we're invited to the wedding!' she said with a wink.

'Ooh, me too,' Jas agreed. 'I'm *so* pleased we finally managed to solve *The Case of the Suspicious Supermodel*!'

'With a little help from Charlie and Joe,' Becky pointed out.

'And Sparky!' Mia added with a smile.

Read on for a special bonus
extract from

THE CASE

of the Haunted Hotel

The
Mayfair
Mysteries

On Friday, Lauren was twice told off at school for not paying attention. All she could think about was that night. She was excited, because it was always fun to have a sleepover with Mia, Becky and Jas, but she was a bit apprehensive too. It wasn't that she really believed that the hotel was haunted, but . . . well, what if something did happen?

That evening she headed off to the mansion wing, loaded down with packets of snacks and bottles of fizzy drinks, as well as her night things. She'd already picked up the key to the Cavalier room from Reception. Mia, Becky and Jas were due to arrive at seven o'clock, and it was only quarter to. For now, Lauren was on her own.

She looked around the room. It was gorgeously decorated in deep red and gold, with the bed covered in a thick velvet throw. The red carpet was so deep that she almost had to wade through it! Framed pictures on the wall showed a girl with ringlets and a bearded man wearing a huge plumed hat. Lauren opened the wardrobe, looked under the bed and peered into all the drawers, just like Charlie had done earlier, but there was nothing that might make ghostly noises.

Built into one wall was a large stone fireplace. Lauren knew that it was hundreds of years old and had been carefully restored by the builders, but the chimney it led to was blocked off. An arrangement of dried flowers and grasses stood in the grate. She wondered if something had somehow got into the chimney – a bird, perhaps – and that was what had caused the spooky sounds that had scared Miss Sharp. The more she thought about it, the more she was convinced she'd solved the mystery, and she felt very cheerful as she put all the snacks into bowls on the dressing table. She didn't even jump when there was a loud knock on the door.

Lauren's dad was outside in the corridor, with Mia, Becky and Jas. 'Your visitors have arrived, Miss Bond,' he said formally, as though he were an old-fashioned butler, and ushered the girls into the room. They thanked him and went in, dumping their bags in a corner.

'Well, I'll leave you to it,' said Mr Bond. 'But remember – if you hear anything at all, you're to call me, all right?'

'Yes, Dad,' Lauren agreed.

Once they were alone, she poured out lemonade for everyone. Jas sat on the bed and started to bounce up and down on it, and Mia handed round the snacks.

Becky, always organized, was unpacking her bag, neatly laying out pyjamas, flannel, soap, toothbrush and toothpaste. Jas slapped her forehead. 'Oh no! I knew there was something I forgot,' she cried.

'It's all right,' said Becky, 'you can use my toothpaste.'

'No – I mean, I forgot everything! I didn't even bring my pyjamas!'

Lauren glanced at Jas's rucksack, still lying in the corner. It looked full to bursting. 'What's in your bag, then?' she asked.

Grinning, Jas picked up her bag and upturned it. Books and candles spilled out onto the bed. 'For atmosphere!' she said.

Mia picked up one of the books. '*Great Ghost Stories*,' she read. 'Oh, Jas, I'm not sure I like the sound of that.'

'Come on, we've got to get into the mood,' said Jas. 'Ghosts! Ghouls! Spooks!'

Lauren realized she hadn't told them her theory about the chimney. She quickly explained. Becky nodded in agreement, and Mia looked relieved. Only Jas seemed disappointed.

'Never mind,' said Lauren. 'Even if the ghost isn't real, it's still got us a sleepover in one of the nicest rooms in the hotel.'

She left the others arranging the candles around the room, and hurried back up to the Bonds' flat to fetch a pair of pyjamas and a toothbrush for Jas to borrow. When she got back, Mia was trying to stick her head up the chimney. 'What are you doing?' Lauren cried. 'Has something happened?'

'No,' said Jas. 'Mia just got worried that the bird or whatever it was might be stuck up there still.'

Mia emerged, brushing dust off her T-shirt. 'I can't see anything up there,' she said, 'or hear anything, either.'

'If it was a bird,' said Lauren, 'it probably found its way out again.'

They'd promised Mr Bond to be in bed by nine o'clock, but even though it was only half past seven they decided to put on their night clothes and get cosy. Everyone laughed when Jas put on Lauren's pyjamas – they barely reached her ankles. 'I didn't realize you were that much taller than me!' Lauren said.

Becky and Jas were sharing the bed, while Mia and Lauren had sleeping bags and lots of cushions on the floor. Becky lit the candles. 'I'll turn the main light off,' she said.

As she flicked the switch, Mia gasped. 'What is it?' Lauren asked.

Mia laughed, embarrassed. 'Just that picture,' she said, pointing at the portrait of the bearded man in his broad-brimmed, feathered hat. 'When the candlelight flickered, it looked like he was blinking . . .'

'Wooooooo!' said Jas in a ghostly voice, as the others joined in Mia's laughter.

'That's a portrait of a Cavalier,' Lauren told Mia. 'This wing was built in 1650, during the English Civil War, when the Cavaliers and Roundheads were fighting each other.'

'Ooh!' cried Jas. 'There's a story about them in one of my books!' She sorted through the pile, finally producing a volume called *Fantastic Phantoms* in triumph. 'Here we go. "The Cavalier's Revenge." Are you sitting comfortably?'

'Yes, Jas!' chorused the others.

'Hold on, I'm trying to get enough light to

read it . . . Here we go, then . . . *"During the time of the English Civil War, Robert Fitzwilliam met and fell in love with beautiful Lady Alice Trelawney, but her parents did not approve of the match. Robert, a supporter of King Charles the First, was being hunted by Oliver Cromwell's Roundheads. He made his way to the Trelawneys' house, but the Roundheads followed him. However Lady Alice, without her parents' knowledge, hid him in a priest hole."'*

'What's a priest hole?' asked Mia.

Becky explained. 'It's a secret chamber built for people to hide in.'

'That's right,' said Jas. 'Listen: "The priest hole was only just big enough for Robert to stand up in, but he knew he'd have to stay there until the Roundheads had moved on. Lady Alice promised to fetch him as soon as it was safe. The Roundheads searched the house from top to bottom, but the priest hole was too well hidden for them to find. Finally they left. But the strain had been too much for Lady Alice, who fainted. She was carried to her bed and remained there in a fever for over a week. When she recovered, she ran straight away to the priest hole. But Robert, not daring to leave the chamber in case the Roundheads were still in the house, had died of thirst!"'

'Oh no!' gasped Mia. 'That's horrible!'

'There's more,' said Jas, turning the page. '"Lady Alice was so horrified that she threw herself down a well! Ever since then, visitors to the house have heard her ghostly wails as she calls out to the man she loves, begging him to forgive her."'

'That's so sad!' said Lauren.

Mia looked up again at the portrait of the Cavalier. 'Robert Fitzwilliam must have looked just like that,' she said. 'And that one' – she turned to the picture of the ringletted girl – 'would be like Lady Alice Trelawney.'

Jas put a white towel over her head. 'Who wanders through the house going *woooo . . . woooo . . . woooo . . .*'

'Woooooooooooooo . . .'

'What was that?' gasped Mia.

'It wasn't me!' said Jas.

'Woooooooooooo . . .'

The girls looked at each other in horror. Where was that ghostly wailing coming from?!